Secrets Under the Skin

Secrets Under the Skin

Hope Hill

and

N. J. Hanson

Ink Drop Press
Chico, California

Secrets Under the Skin

ISBN 13: 978-1-947583-08-5
ISBN 10: 1-947583-08-5

Printed in the United States of America
Cover copyright by Ink Drop Press
Cover design by N. J. Hanson. Cover illustrations by Steve Ferchaud.

To Hope's nieces and nephews: Angelo, Gino, and Arieanna.

And to Nick's nieces and nephews: Entegra, Inara, Braken, Braddock, and Brander.

Chapter One

In the lives of many people, a simple phrase will constantly hang over their heads and torment their subconscious. That phrase is "if only." These two words can dig into a person's mind and bury them to fester like a wound. If only I had taken that job. If only I had asked that girl out in college. If only I hadn't tried to rush the stop light. So many unforeseen possibilities and unfulfilled outcomes. For most people with these regrets, the thought comes later in life, after they've had enough time to reflect on decisions and choices they've made for better or worse. But for Jocelyne "Jocy" Chambers, the first instance of the thought "if only" came when she was just seven years old.

It was the middle of August. With only a few days left of summer vacation for Jocelyne, this was to be their last outing before she started second grade. So when Mom and Dad went on one of their many business trips, they left some money for the babysitter to take the kids on a day trip. The babysitter, Lisa, had asked them what they wanted to do and the three children had collectively agreed. They wanted to go to the Pacific Bay Aquarium. There was a new exhibit, one that would only be open for a few months due to the high maintenance of its main attraction.

At least, that's what the boys wanted. Jocelyne had always felt drawn to the water and loved the aquarium, but the new attraction frightened her.

Her fingers tightened around the hand of her babysitter as they walked into the glass-domed Ocean Tunnel. Above them, held off by nearly four inches of glass with a reinforced steel frame, was a 4.2 million gallon tank teaming with sea life. Jocelyne and her twin brothers gazed up in awe and amazement. Sunlight danced through the water above, creating a ripple effect on the glass as schools of fish swam overhead. A giant sea turtle flapped its flippers like an underwater bird gliding through the water. Nearby, a large ray did the same, diving down to the glass tunnel before swooping away. There were cries of delight and excitement from the gathered crowd.

Suddenly a shadow fell over the tunnel. For a moment, something large came between her and the sun. Jocelyne craned her head back to see and was filled with a level of fear her brain could hardly comprehend. Swimming directly above them, with its massive crescent-shaped tail swishing back and forth to push it along, was what they had come to see. A great white shark.

" 'Mazing!" Travis, one of the twins, shouted in delight. He was younger, only four at the time, and to him sharks where the coolest thing in the world. He ran to the edge of the tunnel and pressed his hands and face against the glass, straining to get a better look. His brother, Jacob, was right at his side. "You see? You see?!" He pointed up at the enormous fish as it swam overhead, stretching his arm out leaning so far forward it looked like he'd tip over.

"Yes, I see," their babysitter, a nineteen year old college girl named Lisa, smiled. "Looks a little scary to me." She looked down to Jocelyne still clutching her hand. "Is it scary to you?"

"Yeah," Jocelyne said without taking her eyes off the shark. "Cool, but a bit scary." She didn't want her fear to show. She wanted to appear strong, she was a big girl after all, and hated being doted upon. Still, there was something about the shark that made her skin crawl, something deep and primal. An instinctual terror she could barely understand. She wished Mom and Dad could be with them, but like usual, they couldn't make it.

An announcer's voice came over the speakers in the tunnel. "Our Pacific Bay Aquarium houses the only great white in captivity," the voice said. "She's a juvenile female, about five and a half feet long and weighing almost a hundred and fifty pounds. In the wild, great white sharks can reach lengths of nearly twenty-one feet and weigh over two tons."

The way the announcer talked about it made the shark seem small, and for a great white it might be, but to a seven-year-old it looked huge, and mean.

The twins moved a little further down the walkway, following the shadow of the shark as it moved overhead. "I want to see it better!" Travis shouted, pushing Jacob aside.

"No, I want to see it better!" Jacob shoved back.

Jocelyne held Lisa's hand tighter. "You alright?" The babysitter asked.

"A little more scared than I thought," Jocelyne admitted, sheepishly.

Lisa crouched down beside Jocelyne. "Hey, it's alright to be scared. It's a big, scary animal. But it's perfectly safe. Sharks are more afraid of people than we are of them."

Her words did little to calm Jocelyne. "Can we go now?" she asked. "I wanna see something else. I wanna see the seals."

"Alright." Lisa took her hand again. "Let's just get your brothers." She called out their names as she stood. "Travis! Jacob!" Then she turned to look down the hall and found the twins gone. A different family stood where they had been, but the boys were missing.

The babysitter turned around in a circle, looking this way and that, but found no sign of the twins. Jocelyne looked around as well, but she also couldn't see them.

"Did you see where they went?"

Jocelyne shook her head.

"Oh, jeez." Lisa pressed a hand against her face, her eyes shut in frustration. "We're going to have to look for them. They can't have gotten far." She took Jocelyne by the hand and they moved out of the underwater tunnel in the last direction the boys went. They entered the jellyfish display, rows of illuminated tubes filled with water and listless drifting jellies. Lisa moved Jocelyne over to a corner. "Stay right here. I'm going to ask a few people if they've seen your brothers."

The babysitter headed off into the crowd, leaving Jocelyne alone. The little girl placed her hands behind her back and started rocking back and forth on her heels. Here, away from the shark, she felt a little better. No longer afraid. She craned her head around, looking up at the ceiling, the far wall, the tubes full of jellyfish.

Along the far wall, a door stood partially ajar. A mop bucket and a push cart full of cleaning supplies and trash bags propped it open. There was a red sign on the door that Jocelyne couldn't read, but she knew people weren't supposed to go through it unless they worked here.

And that's exactly something her brothers would do. Jocelyne glanced back to where Lisa was talking with one of the other visitors, saw the babysitter was distracted, and moved away from the corner. She cracked the door open just enough to see inside, slipped between the door and the janitor cart, and set the door behind her. A tall, metal staircase wound its way back and forth towards the ceiling. Staring straight up, Jocelyne could see two small figures racing each other upwards.

"Hey!" She cupped her hands around her mouth and shouted. "Jacob! Travis!" Her voice carried and the two figures must've heard because they stopped and looked down to her. "We aren't supposed to be back here! Get down!"

They heard, but did not listen. The twins sprinted further up the stairs and Jocelyne could hear their mocking laughter. She took off after them, scaling the staircase as fast as she could. The boys reached the top and opened a door, bright yellow sunlight flooded in just as they raced out and slammed the door behind them.

Jocelyne came to the door and pulled it open. On the other side was a long, narrow walkway twelve feet above the surface of the open sea exhibit. She froze by the door, standing on the metal grate and staring down at the water below. It lapped against the sides of the tank, creating small crests of white foam.

The twins sat in the middle of the walkway, clutching the white poles of the railings with their legs dangling over the edges. They were laughing, pointing out the various fish they could see to one another. "Travis! Jacob!" Jocelyne shouted again, her hands clutched the handle of the door like a vice, afraid to let go. "Come back right now! We're gonna get in trouble!"

"Come over!" Travis waved to her. "Sissy, come look!" The sea turtle breached the surface, its nose rising above the waves and spraying water from the nostrils, before slipping back beneath the waves.

But the turtle wasn't what caught Jocelyne's attention. Just then, a slate-gray triangle sliced through the water's surface like a knife. It swam under the walkway, a massive gray torpedo gliding through the water like a plane through the air. It passed under the boys' shadows. Travis and Jacob jumped to their feet, still clinging to the railing bars, and screaming in delight. Their shoes squeaked on the wet walkway. "So cool!" Travis squealed.

"Come on, guys!" Jocelyne's voice strained. "This isn't funny!" She was terrified, to walk out there and get them.

That fish, that enormous shark, perhaps small by great white standards, was nonetheless a monster compared to them. And it was right there, just a short jump or fall from the walkway to the water. Sure, there was a railing in place to keep people from falling in, but it was designed for adults, not little kids. The top of Jocelyne's head barely reached it, and her brothers had to stretch just to touch the top bar of the rails.

There was a swish of the shark's tail as it dove. The fin slipped beneath the surface, and Jocelyne felt relief. She let out the breath she didn't know she'd been holding.

"Hey! You kids!" A voice split the air. Jocelyne felt her heart seem to jump into her throat and she clutched to the door again.

It was one of the aquarium employees. He was at the far side of the walkway with a walkie-talkie at his belt, a visor shielding his eyes, and a bucket of blood and chopped up fish in one hand. "You can't be over there!"

At that moment came a sight Jocelyne would never forget as long as she lived. The twins jolted to their feet and spun in the direction of the voice, but Travis's shoe slipped on the slick, wet metal and he pivoted to the left. His arms flailed in a desperate attempt to grab something, anything, to steady himself, but he only caught empty air. Jacob reached for his brother, but it was too late. Travis fell screaming, and plummeted into the cold water of the shark tank.

Jocelyne felt like screaming, but found she couldn't. Her throat had clamped shut on itself. Her body felt numb, her hands and fingers cold as ice. Jacob was screaming at the water below, tears streaming down his face with his arms outstretched for his twin. Travis was shouting as well, kicking and paddling as best he could and reaching up to the walkway, but there was no way he could reach it. The park employee rushed onto the narrow bridge with his walkie-talkie raised to his lips. He shouted into the speaker, but Jocelyne couldn't hear what he said. She saw the bucket of fish bait left on the far side of the tank and realized what it meant; this was feeding time.

The dark shape in the water turned and headed back towards the walkway, back towards Travis still treading water. Its tail swished faster, and the triangular fin dipped beneath the surface as the predator dove, preparing to strike its prey. Jocelyne could only watch in horror as the shark moved with a blinding speed toward her brother. Travis shrieked and tried to swim away, kicked and flailing his arms and legs, but the shark was undeterred.

Jocelyne could see its black and empty eyes roll back to white as it closed in. Its jaws seemed to leap from its mouth, an impossible number of teeth reached out, and clamped around Travis's right leg below the knee. Teeth sank into the flesh and blood sprayed out in spurts, turning the water red.

Travis had no time to scream before the shark dragged him underwater, pulling the struggling four year old deeper.

Jacob was crying, lying on his belly with both arms stretched out for his brother, tears streaming down his face and mouth fixed open in a wailing scream. The worker moved frantically back and forth on the walkway, shouting into his radio. There was nothing either of them could do. With every second that passed, the shark took Travis deeper into the tank and the boy lost more blood. In less than a minute, he would be dead.

Before she realized it, Jocelyne caught herself running forward. Her grip on the door handle released and she raced to the edge of the walking platform. She didn't stop when her foot reached the ledge, instead leaping off and holding her arms out before her like a professional swimmer. She dove headfirst, breaking through the water's surface.

She'd closed her eyes before hitting the water, but once beneath the waves she found her vision as clear as crystal. A trail of blood led down to the shark swimming away with her little brother. She gave chase, holding her legs together and moving her body in an up and down fashion like a dolphin.

She swam faster than should be possible, her hair streaming behind her like in a wind tunnel. Her brother dangled listless from the shark's mouth, his arms floating at his side, eyes closed, and mouth dumbly open. Small bubbles drifted up from between his lips. He was alive. Had to be alive. All her thoughts focused on that. So much so, she didn't notice the slight movement of the shark's black eye as she approached.

The shark released its hold on the boy's leg just as Jocelyne reached for his hand. The fish spun around with its jaws open, prepared to render flesh and bone, and snapped at her. Jocelyne twisted in the water as though it were second nature, gracefully dodging the razor sharp, serrated teeth as they closed around nothing. She moved towards Travis's drifting body again, but the shark came for her. Its eyes rolled back as it lunged for her, teeth snapping and gnashing. Jocelyne swam, as the predatory fish gave chase.

Her lungs started to ache. She did not know how long she'd been holding her breath, it could have been only a few minutes, but it felt like forever. They burned as she struggled to keep ahead of the pursuing shark.

She burst through the surface and gasped for air. In that second, she saw the gathering of aquarium workers and employees on the walkway over the tank and along the sides of the tank, all of them staring in shock at this little girl. Jocelyne didn't have much time to process these thoughts, as the great white exploded up from the water right beside her with its jaws fully extended.

Jocelyne took a deep breath and dove, kicking her legs up and down as hard as she could. She found her brother sinking closer to the bottom, the once vibrant trail of red seeping from the missing chunk in his leg was all but gone. She brought her arms around him, cradling the boy against her chest, and pushed off from the bottom. As she rose, the shark descended towards them.

It was coming so fast, a sleek, gray missile homing in on its target. Eyes rolled back once again and mouth opened.

There was no time to dodge. She was rising too fast to move. Jocelyne did the only thing her frightened seven-year-old mind could think to do; she screamed.

Her voice came out like a high-pitched, powerful shriek. A siren wail that vibrated through the water like a sonic wave. Schools of fish froze, stunned, sting rays slowed to a drift, and even the sea turtle turned in her direction. And the shark, the deadly, powerful, great white came to a stop. Its jaws closed slow and harmless, its eyes shifting from rolled back and white to the empty glossy black.

A moment passed while Jocelyne clutched her brother close and the shark seemed to study her. The eyes that were once empty and devoid of thought, now appeared to hold a glimmer of intelligence. Had that been there before and she didn't notice? With a swish of its tail, the great white turned and swam away.

Jocelyne watched it go, then started kicking again. She pushed herself forward, rushing to the surface with her little brother in her arms. She shut her eyes just as they breached, the water bursting around them in an enormous spray that caught the sunlight and cast rainbows before it settled.

She stretched out with one arm and caught the side rail of the walkway as she came down. The combined weight of her and Travis wrenched on her shoulder and she cried out in pain. The aquarium workers pulled both her and her brother up, one had a pair of towels and proceeded to dry them off. Another took a bandanna from his neck and tied it around Travis's knee to help slow the bleeding.

They checked his pulse and were relieved, as well as quite shocked, to find he still had one. They began compressing his chest and forced the water from his lungs, allowing him to breathe again. Once he was stable enough to move, the workers carried him with delicate care to the team of paramedics with a gurney on the far side of the tank.

As they wheeled him away, both Jacob and a soaking wet Jocelyne in tow, a whole new level of anxiety came over her. Was he going to be alright? She had managed to pull him from the mouth of the shark and bring him to safety, but was it enough? After all that, would he die anyway?

If only we hadn't come here, Jocelyne thought. *If only we'd gone to Chuck E. Cheese instead, or to see a movie. If only I hadn't lost sight of them. If only . . .*

Something else came to her. Everything that just happened, what she just did by diving in and saving her brother, was not normal. How could she swim that fast? Or see that well underwater? And that scream, that desperate cry for help that stunned the shark long enough for her to get away, how did she do that?

Jocelyne stared back at the shifting waters of the open sea exhibit tank and pulled the towel tighter around her shoulders. The slate gray, triangular fin rose above the waves just ten feet from where she stood before slipping beneath the surface again.

Chapter Two

Travis's leg had to be amputated below the knee. A large chunk of muscle had been torn away by the shark, leaving the white bone exposed. There was no way to save it.

Public outcry bombarded the Pacific Bay Aquarium for allowing the incident, what the press later called the "Aquarium Shark Attack". The janitor who propped the door open with his cleaning cart while he took a smoke break was promptly fired. The aquarium paid Travis's hospital bills, and their parents opted not to press charges.

The on-site ichthyologist and shark expert determined the attack was brought on by stress-induced aggression caused by the animal being trapped in an enclosure it was rapidly outgrowing, and the shark was simply lashing out at the first thing it saw. As such, the shark was released back into the open ocean two months ahead of schedule.

As for the children involved, not all the scars were as obvious as Travis's missing leg. In the months following the attack, and even after Travis's long stay in the hospital, the twins would wake up three or even four times a night from horrific dreams involving a killer shark. The nightmares plagued Jocelyne for even longer. Perhaps because she was older, her brain was better able to contextualize what happened, and just how close she came to death that day.

But life goes on. Years passed and the family moved up and down the California coast, from the northern forest of Crescent City all the way down to San Diego. They never stayed in one place for too long, two years was the current record. By the time Jocelyne was in her first year of high school, they had settled in a town about an hour north of San Francisco. Their school year had come to an end.

The final school bell rang. Chairs scraped against the floor as the class stood for the last time. It was done. This long, miserable school year was finally over, and for Jocelyne it could not have come sooner. She placed her last text book on the teacher's desk along with the rest of the students and shuffled out of the classroom with her now empty backpack draped over one shoulder.

"Have a nice summer vacation," the teacher, who looked about as tired and ready for the year to be over as they did, chimed in with a weak smile. "I look forward to seeing you next year."

"But you won't," Jocelyne muttered to herself, "and I'm glad for that." This school, like so many of the ones before it, had been rough for her and her brothers. Adjusting to a new school is always difficult, under the best of circumstances, but even more so for them.

In Jocelyne's case, it was the teachers that gave her a hard time. When she showed up on the first day of school with streaks of teal-green in her otherwise sandy blonde hair, the staff listed her as a delinquent and troublemaker from the start and treated her as such. It did no good whenever she tried explaining it was her natural color, no one wanted to hear that. She would get stopped and checked on the mandatory locker and bag check days. There was at least one a month, and the teachers would single her out whenever they wanted to make an example.

It was the same at every school they moved to. Eventually, she stopped trying to correct them and chose to embrace it. If they thought she was a problem kid, might as well not disappoint them. Besides, it didn't matter in the long run, she'd be at a different school next year anyway.

For the twins, it was their fellow classmates that caused problems. With every new school they had to explain again why Travis was missing half his right leg and needed to walk with a prosthetic. The shark had torn enough flesh from his leg to expose bone, so everything from the knee down had to be amputated. Some kids found it cool and exciting. They would clamor around and bombard him with questions about the attack and of the shark, which would cause flashbacks and panic attacks. He'd start screaming again, clam up, hyperventilate, try to hide, and eventually have to be led away.

The other kids couldn't understand. Having to draw their own conclusions, the children assumed he was being stuck up and didn't want to talk with them. Soon, the twins became targets for bullies. Jacob would try to protect his brother, but it always ended in a fight, and a fist fight with a handicapped kid never ended well. None of this helped Jocelyne either, as she stepped in to defend her brothers every chance she got. The problem with that was the kids picking on the twins were usually the same age as Travis and Jacob, three years younger than Jocelyne. No matter the circumstance, no one accepted a sixth grader punching a third grader in the face. So her reputation as a troubled child grew.

Jocelyne brushed a strand of teal-green hair away from her face and hooked it behind an ear. A few steps later, it slipped out and fell over her eyes again. It always did. She stepped out of the broad, double doors of Parkview High, her empty backpack hanging lazily off one shoulder, and headed towards the elementary school. The boys were both eleven years old and just finished sixth grade while Jocelyne was fourteen. This was the first year they didn't go to the same school.

She walked the three blocks to the boy's school and stopped at the street corner she was supposed to meet the twins. They weren't here yet. Feeling restless, she slipped the backpack off, sat on the curb and pulled her phone from the front pocket of her pack. Her thumbs tapped across the screen as she typed out a quick text for her brothers.

Hey, waiting for you at the street corner. Where are you guys?

Once the text was sent, she cupped the phone in her hands and rested her arms over her knees to wait.

Cars drove up and down the street. The tuft of hair fell before her eyes again. Instead of pushing it behind her ear with her hand this time, she stuck out her lower lip and blew it away. An anxious finger tapped against the back of her phone, waiting for a response. She checked the time read-out, two minutes since her text was sent and no reply.

She continued to wait, occasionally checking the time. The longer she sat on the street curb the more annoyed and anxious she became. Some days she thought Jacob and Travis practically lived on their phones, so the idea that they hadn't seen her text was ridiculous. Her leg started bouncing with impatience and she flicked the same lock of hair away from her face.

Once fifteen minutes had past, she slipped the phone back in her pack, slapped her hands on her knees, and shoved herself up off the sidewalk. The boys were sometimes late, but never by this much. And the fact that they hadn't texted back only gave her greater concern. She tugged the straps of her backpack over her shoulders again and crossed the road to the elementary school.

Her first instinct was to head for the office. They boys might be stuck in detention or held after for some other reason and the receptionist could tell her what was up. But as she approached a sound caught her attention. A thump followed by a pained groan. Her hand remained stretched out, hovered above the door handle to the office, as she tilted her head to listen. She soon heard voices.

"Looks like you dropped something, zit face." The first voice taunted.

"Give that back!" The second voice was her brother, Travis. She heard another scruff and something hit the ground along with her brother's distressed cry. "Oaf!"

"Come on, twat!" The first voice said again. "If you want it back, just come get it."

Jocelyne knew who that voice belonged to, and groaned with annoyance. His name was Zackery Taylor, a seventh grader and a particularly buggery little brat. He'd caused near constant torment to Jacob and Travis throughout the year, targeting them whenever he got the chance for no other reason than they were the new kids he could make fun off.

She left the office door without opening it and followed the voices. Rounding the corner, she saw Travis lying on the ground with Zackery standing over him. The older boy held Travis's prosthetic leg over his head, he rattled it back and forth, laughing. "If you want it so much, all you have to do is take it back."

Travis tried to stand, balancing precariously one one foot, and made a grab for his leg. Zackery pulled his arm back so it hung just out of reach. He was two years older than the twins and a good five inches taller. No matter how hard Travis tried, he couldn't reach.

Glancing to the left, Jocelyne spotted Jacob. His arms were held on either side by two more sixth graders. She knew their names, too, Frank and Henry. They followed Zack around like his personal minions and did his bidding when asked. Not particularly smart, just followers using Travis as leverage to torment Jacob.

Zack pressed his free hand against Travis' chest and shoved him back to the ground where the younger boy landed with a painful thud against the concrete. "Is that it? You're gonna have to try harder." He swung the fake leg back and forth casually. "I guess you really don't want it back after all."

Jacob struggled against Frank and Henry's grip. "Stop it!" He spat. "Is this what gets you off? Just because you're dad's rich, you think you can get away with picking on us?"

Zackery glanced over at Jacob. He set the leg over his shoulder like a logger might set their axe, and twisted his lips. "I do it because I want to." He swung the leg around and hit Jacob across the face. A loud smack echoed through the air.

"No!" Travis screamed. He tried to get up again, but Zackery shoved him back down.

"I'll get back to you in a minute." Zackery raised the prosthetic leg again and brought the foot down on Jacob's head again. Over and over, the sixth grader hit the younger boy. Jacob's lip split and a trail of blood spilled down his chin.

"Stop it," Travis tried to protest, but his voice was weak and quiet. "Please." Tears started to flow down his cheeks. "Please, stop. You're hurting him."

"Aww, what's this?" Zack said, leaning down close. "Is baby gonna cry? I'm not hurting him. This is your foot, isn't it? So, really, you're hurting your brother." He hit Jacob with the prosthetic again. "Stop kicking your brother. Stop kicking your brother." He repeated the taunt, hitting Jacob every time he did.

Travis watched the scene transpire before him with solemn defeat in his eyes. There was nothing he could do to stop them or help his brother.

But Jocelyne could. She pulled the backpack off her shoulders, her fingers gripped around the straps in a fist so strong her arm shook, and started marching towards them. One of the other kids, Henry, glanced up to see her approach. "Hey, 'Z'," he said and motioned his head in her direction.

Zack turned, then laughed when he saw her. "Look at this! Big sis has decided to save your sorry butt."

Jocelyne gave his taunts no notice.

Her lips twisted in a sneer and brows furled in a glare so full of rage, she thought she might set things on fire if she stared hard enough. She tossed the backpack aside, then slammed her fist into her open palm with a thwacking sound. The same noise Travis's prosthetic leg made when Zackery hit Jacob. The same sound her fist would make when it connected with their faces. Her knuckles popped.

"Hey, what's up?" Zack said with a nervous chuckle. He tossed the leg to the ground, held his arms at his side and took a step back. "What you gonna do, beat me up? When my dad hears about this, you'll be lucky if your parents can afford to rent a spot in the trailer park."

Jocelyne ignored his weak taunts. If Zack wanted to go crying to his dad about how he was afraid of a girl after picking on a disabled kid, that was his prerogative, but Jocelyne didn't need some grown up to settle things for her. She was more than capable of handling things herself.

Without saying a word, Jocelyne's slow walk became a sprint. She closed the distance between herself and the bully in a matter of seconds, giving Zackery no time to react before her fist struck his face.

He stumbled back, reeling from the impact, and tripping over his own feet. Before he could recover, Jocelyne punched him again. Zack clasped both hands over his face as he groaned in pain. He pulled his hands away and saw the smears of red on his palms, blood trickled down from his nostrils. "You broke my nose, you bi–"

Jocelyne slammed her hands down on his shoulders and brought her knee up sharply to bash against his groin. Zack's eyes seemed to bulge from his face. He fell to his knees, clutching at his wounded pride. Only a weak, pathetic squeak escaped his throat. She then threw him to the ground, sat on his chest with her knees pressed down on his arms, and wrapped her hands around his throat.

Zack gagged. He struggled and kicked, but couldn't move enough to dislodge her. Jocelyne's grip tightened. She watched with a twisted sense of glee as Zack's face reddened and his eyes grew wide, veins throbbing in his neck. No one moved to stop her, Zack's two cronies were too shocked and frightened to step in, afraid they might be next, and the twins could hardly believe they were watching their sister strangle a guy.

Her heart leapt with surprise as a pair of arms looped around her waist and pulled her back. They wove around her shoulders and two large, powerful hands clasped behind her head. A part of her brain recognized it as a full nelson, but mostly she was shocked and angry at being dragged away. "Let me go!" She screamed.

"That's enough, young lady!" The voice was loud and booming beside her ear. The elementary school principal lifted her away with ease, keeping her in the head lock as she struggled. "You will calm down, or I will keep you like this until your parents arrive. Or the police, I'm not sure which one I should call."

Jocelyne snorted, but stopped thrashing. After a few moments, the principal released his hold. She lurched forward, taking a few steps to steady herself, before turning to face the livid school staff member.

"Is this anyway to act on the last day?" The principal, Mr.

Hernandez, folded his arms across his chest. He was a tall man, easily reaching six feet, and muscularly built supporting the rumor that he used to be a football player. He wore a blue, button-up shirt with the sleeves rolled up to his elbows under a black tie and vest. His short goatee and hair, once fully black, had started to gray around the edges from years of dealing with unruly students and their parents. "Is this just a thing for you, beating and strangling those younger than you?"

"I was defending my brothers!" Jocelyne shouted. "This sleazebag was pushing them around, destroying his things, and generally being a grade-A asshole!"

"Watch that language, young lady." Mr. Hernandez pointed at her.

"What are you going to do if I don't?" She continued. "Clearly you don't give a rat's ass what people do at your school, since these guys were messing with my brothers right outside your office and you did nothing about it. What kind of school are you running where jackasses are allowed to pick on handicapped kids!?"

"We weren't doing anything like that." Zack's said in a strained voice as he got to his feet, his hand rubbing at his sore throat. With any luck, there would be finger-shaped bruises there tomorrow. "We were just helping them get their stuff together when this crazy girl attacks me from out of nowhere. I think they set me up to jump me."

"Be quiet." Mr. Hernandez glared over his shoulder at Zackery. "I wasn't born yesterday. I know you well enough to know when you're the cause." He turned back to Jocelyne. "As for you, young lady, I'm going to have a talk with your parents this afternoon. You and your brothers are going to have to wait until they come to pick you up."

"What?" Jocelyne shouted. "On the last day you're going to make us stay after?"

"Should've thought of that before you decided to choke someone half to death." The principal said. Zackery shot her a slimy smirk, the blood still dripped down his face from his broken nose. "Same thing for you, young man." Mr. Hernandez turned to face Zack. "You'll be staying to wait for your father and you can explain everything to him."

"What? No!" He stomped his foot on the pavement. "You can't do that! My dad owns this school, he owns all of you! If not for him, you wouldn't have a job!"

"And I'm sure he will be pleased to hear how you used his position to bully a child two years younger than you with a prosthetic leg," Mr. Hernandez said.

Zackery folded his arms and smirked. "He'll never believe you."

"We'll see. Now, all of you, to my office." The principal lead them into the building. He made Jocelyne, Jacob, and Travis sit on one side of the room and Zackery, Henry, and Frank sit on the other.

Jocelyne and Zackery glared at one another. He had a tissue to his face which was already saturated with blood. They said nothing, just shot dirty looks at each other while they listened as the principal in the other room spoke loudly over the phone. First to Jocelyne's parents, and then to Zack's. After what sounded like a long, heated conversation, he set the phone down and stepped into the hallway. "I got a hold of both your fathers." Mr. Hernandez said. "They're both on their way." He took one of the chairs from his office and placed it between the children. "Now, we are going to sit here in silence until they arrive." He sat down, folded his arms, and waited.

Zackery's father was the first to arrive. He stormed into the office fifteen minutes after the phone call with an angry flushed face and rage in his eyes. "What kind of show are you running, Hernandez!?" Mr. Taylor, Zack's father, roared at the principal.

"Is this what you allow? Vicious little monsters from the junior high coming over and beating up my son?"

"Mr. Taylor, as I explained on the phone, your son is not innocent in this case. He hasn't been all year." Mr. Hernandez pushed himself from the chair and stood.

"I don't want to hear it." Mr. Taylor thrust his arm in the direction of his son. "Look at him. Are you telling me that's not the work of a violent, psychotic monster? You think you can try to pin this on my son?"

"No, I don't think. I know. I have footage from the school's security system. If you'd care to review it, we can see what really happened." Mr. Hernandez said.

Zack's face turned white from shock. Jocelyne's eyes also snapped wide open. The security camera! How could she be so stupid as to forget about the camera? It was placed right outside the principal's office overlooking the playground. Directed right where the fight happened!

"I would very much like to see it." Mr. Taylor pushed past the principal as he walked into Mr. Hernandez's office. The door closed behind them, leaving the kids to sit and stew in the hallway. Several minutes later, Zackery's father came back out. He looked over at Jocelyne and her brothers, "I'm sorry for the trouble my son caused you. I will make sure he never does it again." He then grabbed his son by the arm and wrenched him up from the chair. "We will have a talk with your mother, and then I'll decide the appropriate consequence for you."

Mr. Taylor dragged his frightened son out of the building with the boy's two friends right behind. He opened the door just as Jocelyne's father, Benjamin Chambers, stepped inside. The two men exchanged a tense, silent look, then Mr. Taylor left with his son.

Jocelyne felt the heat rising up her neck. She didn't face her father, just stared at the floor with her hands folded in her lap.

"Mr. Chambers," the principal said as he extended his hand, "glad you could make it."

"I'm not." Benjamin Chambers shook Mr. Hernandez's hand. "I don't like meeting under these circumstances. Are my kids in any serious trouble?"

"Well, what can I really do to them on the last day of school?" The principal stated. "But I do have some security footage of what happened if you'd like to see it."

"That's won't be necessary." Jocelyne's father said. He turned back to the kids still sitting in the walkway. "Jocelyne, boys, let's go."

They all stood and collected their bags. Jocelyne swung her empty backpack over her shoulders, still keeping her gaze averted. As they were walking out the door, which their father held for them, Mr. Hernandez spoke again. "Mr. Chambers," he said, "how many times has Jocelyne gotten in trouble for picking fights at school?"

"Are you genuinely asking me, or are you going somewhere with this?" Her dad asked.

"I'll tell you." Hernandez slipped his hands in his pockets. "No less than ten times this year. Ten fights with other students, all of them younger than her."

Jocelyne spun around to face the principal again. "All of them were picking on my brothers!" She snapped. "Maybe if you did your job– "

"Quiet, young lady!" Mr. Chambers shouted. She winced at his raised voice. Her lip quivered and her hands tightened around the straps of her backpack. She felt like crying, but forced her tears back.

"And her relationship with teachers has been strenuous at best." Mr. Hernandez continued.

"I am aware." Jocelyne's father replied. "I will talk with her when we get home."

"Even so, I'm going to recommend her to a counselor. I have someone specific in mind, and he's really good at what he does."

"Thanks, but no thanks." Her father said. "We can handle it ourselves." He stepped away and followed the kids to the car.

Chapter Three

Jocelyne climbed into the front seat while the boys sat together in the back. Dad walked around the car and slid into the driver's side, started the engine, and pulled out of the school's parking lot. They drove home in silence, Jocelyne clutched her backpack on her lap. She'd look over at her father every so often, but only see his stern face staring out the windshield.

"Jocelyne," he said at last, and it felt like a stone dropped in her stomach to hear her own name, "tell me, and be honest, why do you make a scene at every school we move you to?"

"It's not my fault," Jocelyne tried to defend herself, "they'd taken Travis's leg and were pushing him to the ground. And they had Jacob in a hold to stop him from helping."

"I didn't ask about this incident." Dad said. "Why is it, no matter where we go, you always seem to make enemies of your teachers and classmates?"

"I don't know." She turned away to look out the window. "Because they all suck. Because they treat me like crap."

"All of them? In every school? Everyone treats you terribly?" Dad clicked the blinker on and they turned down the street towards their house. "If everyone has a problem with you, maybe you're the problem. The way you act gives them cause to distrust you."

Jocelyne's shoulders hunched and she clutched her empty backpack tighter. She'd heard this all before, and it never helped.

Dad pulled the car into the driveway beside their mother's car and shut off the engine. "Until further notice, you're grounded. No TV, no internet, and no games for a month."

"A month!?" Jocelyne almost jumped from her seat. "But summer just started!"

"You should've thought of that before getting into a fight on your last day of school." Dad pushed his door open and stepped outside.

Jocelyne threw her head back against the seat and groaned before stepping out of the car. The boys followed suit. Travis's prosthetic squeaked and groaned in a way it hadn't before, clearly broken from Zackery using it as a club.

They walked into the house and found Mom standing near the table. Dinner had already been prepared and set out for them. "Honey," she straightened out and smiled, her hands clasped together. "Welcome ho-" she stopped when she saw their solemn looks. Her gaze was especially drawn towards Jacob, whose face was still red and covered with welts and bruises. He had a black eye, and held tissues to his lips to stem the bleeding. "Oh, my goodness!" Mom raced across the room to coddle her son. "My poor baby, what happened? Who did this to you?"

"Mom! Stop! You're embarrassing me." Jacob tried to fend her off, but Mom was too insistent. Jocelyne and Travis smirked as they watched.

"I'm your mother, I'm supposed to." She said, cradling him against her. "When I find out who did this, he's going to have to run home to his own mother."

"You don't have to worry about that." Dad said as he took off his shoes and set them on the rack beside the door. "Jocelyne throttled the other boy pretty good. The principal said he found them with her hands around his throat, pinning the kid to the ground."

"He deserved it." Jocelyne said. She refused to look at either of her parents. She set her shoes beside the door, then slipped her backpack into the hall closet where it would sit for the rest of the summer, or until they moved again, whichever happened first.

"That's beside the point." Dad said. "Now, all of you go wash up and get ready for dinner."

The three siblings took turns in the bathroom washing their hands and faces. Once they were done, they came back to the dining room and helped set the plates, silverware, and glasses on the table.

"It smells delicious," Father said as he pulled out his chair. "What is it?"

"Tonight I made meatloaf, mashed potatoes with gravy, steamed broccoli with melted cheese, and garlic bread." Mom said, a hint of pride in her voice. "I found a new recipe online for the meatloaf."

"It doesn't have onions, does it?" Travis complained. "I hate onions."

"Me, too." Jacob agreed.

"You'll just have to deal with it." Father told them.

A knock came at the door. The clinking and clattering of knives and forks stopped and everyone looked up in confusion.

"Are you expecting anyone, honey?" Mom shifted to face Dad.

"Not that I know of." He replied.

Another series of knocks came from the door. Dad set his fork down, stood up, and answered it. A man stood on the front porch. He wore a gray vest and matching slacks over a red button-up shirt with the sleeves rolled up to passed his elbows. His beard was red, speckled with gray and neatly trimmed. His hair bore the same shade of red. A pair of gold-rimmed spectacles rested on the bridge of his nose. He carried a briefcase in one hand. "Good evening," the man said and Jocelyne could hear a hint of an accent, although she did not know where it was from. "Are you Mr. Ben Chambers?"

"I am," Dad stated, "and I'm not interested in buying anything." He was about to close the door when the strange man placed the toe of his shoe in the way.

"I'm not a salesperson. I'm a counselor," the man said. "My name is Mr. Otto, I specialize in unique cases and troubled youth. I'd like the talk for a little bit with Ms. Jocelyne."

"And as I told the principal, we don't need a counselor. Now, if you don't mind, we're in the middle of dinner." Dad's voice grew more insistent.

Jocelyne leaned forward in her chair, trying to get a better look at the strange man. She couldn't see around her father, though.

"You misunderstand." Mr. Otto reached into his vest pocket and pulled something out. He held it up so her father could see, but Jocelyne still couldn't. "She sent me."

A hushed silence fell over the room. Ben Chambers' eyes grew wide as he stared at the photograph in Mr. Otto's hand. He looked over his shoulder at Shannon, and she soon realized who the counselor spoke of. The same look of shock grew across her face. Jocelyne looked back and forth from her father to her mother, and back again. "What is it?" she asked. "Who sent him?"

"Jocelyne, boys, could you go to your rooms for a minute? We'll come get you when we're done." Dad said.

"What?" Jocelyne jumped to her feet. "That's not fair. I want to hear what he has to say."

"Jocelyne, listen to your father." Mom stated as she rose from the table and started gathering the plates. "Go to your room, please. Just until we're finished talking. Boys, you too."

"Ugh." She scoffed, tossing her utensils on her plate. She stormed off to her room, shoulders hunched, hands stuffed in her jean pockets, and lip pushed out in a pout. Jacob and Travis rose from the table and followed her down the hall. "It's not fair." Jocelyne said as they turned the corner out of sight. "This guy, Mr. Otto, comes here to talk to me, and Mom and Dad force me to leave. What don't they want me to hear?"

"I don't know." Jacob said. "And why do you care? It's probably something to do with the school. You did pick a fight on the last day."

"I was trying to protect you guys." She retorted. "Zack and his toadies were pushing you around and messing you up. What kind of sick jerks pick on a kid with a fake leg? I just stepped in to stop them."

"You got him in a stranglehold and he was starting to pass out." Travis countered. "What kind of person gets in a fight with a kid a year younger than them?"

She rolled her eyes. "Forget it." Jocelyne went into her room and pushed the door so it was open just a sliver. She peered through the gap between the door and the frame, waited until her brothers had shut their own door, then snuck back into the hall.

The hallway formed a T shape, a long shaft that branched out laterally to the kid's bedrooms with a shared bathroom between them. Jocelyne pressed her back against the wall in the shadows as she crept to the corner leading to the living room, where Mom and Dad were talking to Mr. Otto. Peeking around the edge, she saw her parents and the supposed school counselor seated across the table from one another.

"You're saying SHE sent you?" Mom asked, and already Jocelyne's mind was forming questions. Who was this "she" they spoke of? And why would they be sending anyone?

"Yes," Mr. Otto said. His voice was a little different now, with a heavier accent than before, and more natural, like he wasn't trying to disguise it anymore. "I've been trying to find you ever since the aquarium incident."

The aquarium? Jocelyne thought, *But that was years ago. How would he know about that?*

The counselor continued. "How much does she know?"

"About what?" Dad asked. Jocelyne moved closer to the corner, almost in the light from the front room lamps, straining to listen.

"You know what I'm talking about," Mr. Otto said. "About who she is. And what she is."

What I am? Her stomach fluttered as the words reached her ears and settled in her brain. What were they talking about, and what did it all mean? She listened closer.

"We haven't told her anything," Dad said. "And we won't.

Not as long as we can help it."

"That's right," Mom agreed. She reached over the table and took her husband's hand. "We're trying to protect her. If she knows too much . . ." she let the sentence trail off.

If I know too much what? Jocelyne thought.

"You can't hide the truth from her forever," the counselor said. "What are you going to say when the changes start? When she comes into her second skin?"

"We don't even know that it will happen," Dad said, his voice growing more aggravated. "And I don't like what you're insinuating."

"I don't mean to insinuate anything," Mr. Otto stated. He ran a hand across his graying hair. "But you can't deny it for too much longer. I noticed the streak of teal in her hair, which I could tell was natural. That is a sign of her emerging gifts. Her heritage is calling, you know it will happen. The incident with the shark was her awakening, will she be ready for it?"

"If anything occurs, we'll tell her then." The chair scraped across the floor and father stood. "I believe it's time for you to leave."

"I didn't mean to offend. And I apologize if I did." Mr. Otto said as he grabbed his briefcase. "Before I leave, may I use your washroom?"

"Straight down the hall," father said. "I'll show you."

Jocelyne heard their approach. She pushed herself away from the floor and hurried back to her room. Inside, she kept the light off and the door slightly open, just enough to see Dad and the stranger reach the bathroom.

She watched and waited, hearing the flush of the toilet and the running of the sink faucet until the man left the bathroom and father led him back down the hall to the living room. Once they were out of sight, she crept back into the hall and hid by the corner.

The front door closed and father came back to sit at the table beside mother. "Do you think he's telling the truth?" Mom asked.

"Doesn't matter," Father replied. "Our only concern is to keep her safe. We made a promise."

"I know, but what if she discovers on her own?" Mother said. "She's almost fourteen. I was the same age when I had my first change."

"But she's not you," Dad retorted. "It may never happen. And if it doesn't, then we shouldn't bring it up. We'll just forget about it."

"For how long?" Mom said. "We can't hide her real

parentage from her forever."

Jocelyne's fingers covered her lips as she suppressed a gasp. Her eyes grew wide and her heart felt like it had stopped in her chest. Had she just heard what she thought she did? Her real parentage? What did they mean?

"But that's the promise we made to her mother. Her safety is our top priority, and if that means keeping her in the dark, then so be it," father, or the man who called himself her father, said.

All the strength in her legs slipped away. They felt weak and watery, unable to hold her up anymore, and she slid down to the floor. *A promise made to my mother,* she thought. Those words resonated stronger and harsher than any before. Those two people in the living room, the man and woman who had raised her as a daughter and who she regarded as parents, were nothing of the sort.

Her lips quivered and chest heaved as tears formed in the corners of her eyes. Everything she was, all that knew, everything they ever told her, it was all a lie. She wasn't just adopted, they were deliberately keeping things from her. The more that realization settled on her, the less control she had over herself. Soon she would be bawling like a toddler, and she didn't care.

Some part of Jocelyne's mind recognized that if she started crying in the hallway it would alert the boys and probably her fake parents that she'd listened in on their conversation, and that she knew the truth. And while part of her wanted to scream at them, to call them out on all the secrets they've kept and lies they've told, she knew she couldn't deal with the fallout right now. She picked herself up off the floor, still careful to be as silent as possible, and tip-toed to the bathroom.

With the door locked behind her and the shower fan on to drown out any noise, she broke down and sobbed. She folded on the bathroom mat, her arms wrapped around her legs and face buried in her knees, bawling her eyes out. Her whole body shook with each short, choking breath.

After a long while, honestly she couldn't tell how long but it felt like hours, her crying fit stemmed. Jocelyne dried her eyes on a nearby towel. She was still sniffly, but at least she wasn't weeping anymore. She stood up and looked at her reflection in the mirror. Her eyes were red and puffy and lines of warm salty water ran down her cheeks. She turned on the faucet and splashed water on her face, then used the same towel to dry off.

As she looked at the mirror again, she noticed a slip of paper poking out from behind the medicine cabinet. It was lined paper, with a row of freshly torn ridges on one side from a spiral notebook. A large, capital letter "J" written in red ink adorned the page. She opened the cabinet and pulled out the paper, finding a message left by the school counselor.

Dear Jocelyne,

I'm sorry we didn't get to speak much in person. We have much to talk about and I'm sure you're eager to know more. My number is (707) 555-1888. Call or text me so we can arrange a meet up and I can tell you what I know.

Signed, a friend,

Mr. Otto

P.S. Flush this note after you read it so no one finds it.

Jocelyne stood at the bathroom sink for a long time, the paper with its strange note remained clutched in her hands and her eyes never left those red letters. What did he want to talk about that her parental figures didn't want her to know? For that matter, how did he know it?

She reflected on the conversation held between the adults

when they thought she wasn't listening. Mr. Otto mentioned the shark attack at the aquarium, causing Jocelyne to think back on that day. How she dove into the tank to save Travis, how her vision remained clear even in the salt water, and how she swam with speed and power to match any ocean creature. And then, of course, that scream she gave off when the shark came for her. Her desperate scream that placated all the fish and sea life in the tank. Mr. Otto said that moment was her awakening, but to what?

She wanted to know the truth. Mom and Dad would never tell her what they knew, but Mr. Otto might. Jocelyne read over the message several more times, committing the phone number to memory, then crumpled the note into a ball and tossed it in the toilet. She pushed the handle down and watched the paper ball swirl around the bowl before it disappeared down the drain, lost forever. But she had the phone number, and that held the key to the truth or who, or what, she was.

A knock came from the door which made her jump and let out a quiet gasp. "Jocelyne, you've been in there for like an hour!" Jacob's voice came from the other side. She sighed and rolled her eyes. Maybe fifteen minutes, at most, but not an hour. She threw the door open to find him standing in the hallway, staring at her with an angry pout and folded arms. "Finally," he said as he pushed past her, "why do girls always take so long?"

"Sorry," Jocelyne mocked, "I was making sure not to make a mess like you."

She closed the bathroom door and walked back down the hall to her bedroom. Once inside, she quietly locked the door behind her, snatched her phone off the desk, and threw herself on the bed. She opened the message option on her phone and was just about to type out a text when she stopped, her thumbs hovered over the screen with hesitation.

Jocelyne realized she was planning to meet up with a much older man, without her parents knowledge or consent, so he could share some things with her. She thought about it and chuckled a little, realizing this sounded like the set up for some abduction movie where the daughter is kidnapped and the dad has to go all commando to get her back. And if something happened to her, there was no way her dad was ever going to be cool enough to come rescue her.

No, she thought and her smile faded, *not her father.* That man wasn't her real dad and that woman wasn't her real mom. Renewed by this thought, she started a new conversation in her messages, typed up a quick text just saying that she wanted to meet and learn what he had to say, and sent it off to the counselor. She barely had time to set the phone down before a response popped up in her inbox. She opened it.

Ms. Jocelyne Chambers, it is good to hear from you so soon. I'm sure you have many questions, which would be best talked about in person. Is there any place you'd like to meet so we can talk?

Still a little nervous, Jocelyne didn't know what to reply. Her thumbs hovered over the screen, but didn't move. After a few moments of thought, she typed a new message.

I can meet you in the food court at the mall tomorrow morning. I want to know the truth.

She found herself hesitating again. She wanted to send the message, but a part of her still struggled to press the button.

"Jocelyne," Shannon's voice came from the other side of the door, "you can come out, now. The food's getting cold."

"Yeah, just a second." Jocelyne replied. She sent the text.

Chapter Four

Jocelyne couldn't sleep that night, she was too full of twisting thoughts, and mixed emotions. She lay on the bed and stared at the ceiling well into the night, watching the shadows cast by the street lamp dance along her walls. At some point she must've slept, because the next thing she knew her alarm clock was beeping.

She sat up, rubbed the sleep from her eyes, and hit the button on the top of her alarm. She still felt so exhausted. She stumbled down the hall, and made her way to the kitchen. She hadn't meant to wake up this early, and really wouldn't have if she'd remembered to shut her alarm clock off the night before. As it was, she was too distracted by other things and simply forgot about it until the alarm went off that morning.

Still rubbing her eyes awake, Jocelyne came to the kitchen to find Dad sitting at the table concealed behind the morning newspaper and Mom over the stove preparing a big pan of scrambled eggs and a skillet of bacon.

Mom put on a pair of oven mitts and brought the eggs and bacon to the table. As she set them down, she glanced up and saw Jocelyne walking down the hall. "Good morning, Honey," Mom, or rather Shannon Chambers, smiled and waved to her. She set the egg-covered spatula in the pan and moved in to hug Jocelyne. "You're up rather early."

Before Mom could reach her, Jocelyne wove to one side to avoid her. "Yeah, I forgot to shut my alarm off." She said with a scratchy voice. She took a plate from the cupboard and was about to grab the spoon in the eggs when Dad, or rather Ben Chambers, placed the lid over the pan.

"What do you think you're doing, young lady?" He asked.

"Getting breakfast." She said with a groan.

"You're still grounded, remember?" He said. Leaving the eggs covered, he reopened the newspaper. "You know where the cereal is."

Jocelyne narrowed her eyes and snorted. She tossed the plate on the table in a huff, and as she turned to get a bowl from the same cupboard, Ben Chambers cleared his throat. "Is that where that belongs?'

She groaned again, snatched the plate off the table and stuffed it back in the cupboard, then grabbed a bowl. She moved silently through the kitchen, not looking at or otherwise acknowledging the adults, and filled her bowl with cheerios and milk. Once she had her breakfast, she sat opposite Mr. Chambers and started slurping the unsweetened O's from her spoon.

"Eat normally," Ben said without looking away from his newspaper. "Don't slurp your food."

Jocelyne fixed a glare on the back of the newspaper, and then proceeded to slurp the milk louder. The top of the paper slid down so father could look over it. "Jocelyne," he said.

"Honey, please," Shannon interjected, "do as you're told."

"Why?" She said before she could stop herself.

"Excuse me?" Ben was on his feet, the paper folded and set aside, and he focused both his intense eyes on her. "What did you say, young lady?"

Well, you started this, Jocelyne thought. *Time to go big or go home.* "Why should I do as you say?" She brought the bowl to her mouth and drank the rest of the milk.

"Because I'm your father, that's why." Ben towered over her, leaning forward and pointing down at her like she was a dog that just made a mess on the rug. "And you need to quit with this little attitude of yours, or I swear you'll be grounded for the rest of the summer."

No, you're not, Jocelyne thought, but still couldn't bring herself to say. *You're not my real father.* She took her empty bowl and spoon to the sink and as she passed Shannon Chambers, she thought, *And you're not my real mom.* Once the bowl had been rinsed, she placed it and the spoon both in the dishwasher and left the kitchen for her bedroom.

Ben Chambers slumped back in his chair with a sigh and rubbed his forehead with the tips of his fingers as though he had a headache. Give it long enough, he would probably have one for real. "What has gotten into that girl?"

"She's a teenager, of course she's going to have an attitude." Shannon sat beside her husband and placed her hand on his shoulder. "She's just going through a rebellious phase, that's all. Every fourteen-year-old does this. She'll grow out of it, you'll see."

"Yeah," Ben said in a dejected tone, "in another four years."

"If that's how long it takes." Shannon gave him a small kiss on the cheek, and then stood. As she turned away to finish preparing breakfast, her husband spoke to her again.

"I've been thinking," he took his plate and spooned a heaping of eggs onto it. Beside them, he placed three strips of bacon. "About Jocelyne."

"Yes?" Shannon asked.

"It's about what you said the other day." He took his fork, but rather than eat the eggs before him, he poked and prodded at them. "Maybe you were right. We can't keep the truth from her forever. We should tell her."

Ben looked over to Shannon, and found her with her hands clasped together at chest level with wide eyes and a huge smile of delight. "Oh, honey, do you mean it?"

"Yes," Ben said, and couldn't help but smile a little at how adorable she looked. It reminded him of when they first met, all those years ago on his business trip to Scotland. They were both much younger back then, and significantly less stressed. Before they made the promise concerning Jocelyne. "She deserves to know the truth."

Shannon came running back and threw her arms around him. She giggled and kissed him again. "This is wonderful! I can't wait to show her everything and help her with her first transformation. I only wish my sister could be here with her too."

"Let's not get ahead of ourselves yet." Ben commented. "We're still not sure yet if she can change or not. She might not have inherited that."

"With who her parents are, I have no doubts," Shannon said. "When do you want to tell her?"

"I don't know, yet. Some time soon." Ben looked past Shannon's head and saw the stove clock. A sudden rush of adrenaline rushed through him and he jumped to his feet. "Oh, crap! I'm going to be late!" He shoveled his breakfast into his mouth, set the plate down and grabbed his briefcase. "We'll talk more about this when I get home." He gave her a quick kiss, and went out the door.

Jocelyne sat on her bed beside the open window. She listened as the car engine rumbled to life, then pulled out the driveway and grew quieter as it drove away. Once the sound was gone, she smiled and jumped off her bed. It was time.

She pulled off her pajamas, light-blue fleece with yellow seashell print, and threw them onto the floor. She was starting to outgrow them, before the next school year she would need new ones, but right now she didn't care.

She proceeded to dress herself in a pair of faded blue jeans, an off yellow t-shirt, and a red windbreaker. While it was early June, living on the northern California coast meant the weather was still chilly sometimes. She used a brush to straighten her bedhead mess of hair, then grabbed an elastic band to tie it back in a ponytail.

One tuft of her teal streak hung over her eyes. She looked at it with annoyance and tried to push it behind her ear, only for it to fall back in front of her face. This always happened, no matter how much she prepped or brushed, a tuft of teal hair always got loose.

Didn't matter right now. She turned on her bedside radio and cranked the music up loud enough to be heard from the living room, but not too loud. Just enough to make the woman think she was still in her room. She then laced up her shoes and climbed out the bedroom window.

Her bike leaned up against the outside wall of the house, a chain wrapped around the frame and secured it to the back porch. Her helmet rested over one of the handle grips. She fished the key from her pocket and unlocked the chain, then looped it around the center bar of the frame, settled the helmet on her head, hopped onto the seat, and pedaled out of the backyard and down the street.

The wind blew in her face. Her unzipped jacket flapped behind her like a small cape as she rode. Occasionally, a car would pass by and Jocelyne would swerve closer to the sidewalk to avoid them, but for the most part, the streets were empty. She rode on until the large structure of the mall loomed in the distance.

The mall was only a few miles from her house, a short ride on the bike. Even so, her legs ached by the time she got there. She dismounted and locked her bike at the bike rack and left the helmet resting on the handlebars like before.

She went inside and walked down the long hallways, she walked by an endless stream of stores until finally she made it to the food court. The mall was mostly deserted, with only a few people milling about, but that was to be expected at this time in the morning. One of those people, however, was the man she came to see. The school counselor from last night, the one who introduced himself as Mr. Otto, sat at one of the small circular tables with a briefcase beside his leg and a strawberry smoothie in his hands.

Jocelyne approached, both eager and worried at the same

time. She wanted to know the truth, but what if it was a bad truth? What if what he had to say was something she didn't want to hear? Nevertheless, her feet brought her closer.

He looked up from his smoothie and waved when he saw her. "Ah, good morning to ya." He stood and extended his hand. "Nice to meet you for real this time, Ms. Jocelyne Chambers. I'm Mr. Otto."

"Yes, I remember." Jocelyne shook his hand and examined him quickly. He wore gray slacks and a gray vest over a red long sleeve shirt and a matching tie. A pair of gold rimmed spectacles rested on his nose. He had a short, red beard speckled with stray gray whiskers and his hair was likewise cut short and the same shade of red. Much about him was red now that she thought about it.

"Please take a seat." Mr Otto gestured to the seat opposite him. He returned to his own chair and brought the briefcase to the table. "We have a lot to discuss."

"I know." Jocelyne pulled her chair out and sat down.

"Before I begin, tell me a little about yourself." Mr. Otto adjusted his glasses, pushed them up the bridge of his nose.

"Like what?" Jocelyne asked.

"Just simple things." Mr. Otto clarified. "What kind of TV

shows do you like? Have any favorite books or movies? What are some of your hobbies? That sort of thing."

Jocelyne was a little confused. This wasn't what she expected them to talk about. "I thought we were going to talk about secrets." She said.

"We are. But I just want to get a little more information about you. The school only told me you were a problem child with a bit of a temper," Mr. Otto said. "But I believe there's more to you than that. I think there's more you want people to see than just a problem. So, tell me a little about yourself."

Jocelyne blew the tuft of teal hair away from her eyes. "Well, I don't get to watch a lot of TV on my own, our TV is password locked. My favorite movie is this old movie about a mermaid called *Splash*, and my favorite books are the Harry Potter series."

"Oh, really," Mr. Otto said with some surprise. "And what about hobbies?"

"I actually really like to swim." She replied.

"Nice. Do our parents take you to the beach very often?"

"No, not really." Jocelyne admitted.

"Why not? You live right next to it." Mr. Otto stated. "In fact, according to your school records, every town you've transferred from has been on the coast. But you say your parents don't take you to the beach? How come?"

"I don't know," She shrugged her shoulders.

"Uh huh," the counselor nodded in thought. "Thank you, that's what I needed to know."

"Now you'll tell me what the secrets are?"

"Yes. Just let me ask how much you know already." Mr. Otto rested his hands on the locks of the briefcase, but did not open it. "Just so I know I'm not repeating anything."

Jocelyne sighed. Her shoulders felt rigid and her hands folded together on her lap. "Really, I don't know anything," she admitted. "I overheard you talking with my parents – " she caught herself, and then changed her wording, "with the adults at the table last night, but that's all."

"Hm," Mr. Otto's lips pursed. "I see." He leaned forward on his elbows and laced his fingers together in front of his face. "Did they say anything after I left?"

"They mentioned something," Jocelyne said. "A promise they made to my mother."

"Very interesting," Mr. Otto straightened up. "Well, first, let me ask you something." He propped his elbows on the table again. "I want you to remember back to when you were a child.

The day at the aquarium."

"How do you know about that?" Jocelyne narrowed her eyes.

"I heard about it on the news," Mr. Otto said. "Things like that don't happen every day. The Pacific Bay Aquarium had quite a media firestorm after that. And I was a little surprised to learn that your parents," he paused and smiled, "well, adopted parents, chose not to press charges." He straightened up in his chair. "But anyways, I want you to tell me the things the papers never did."

"Like what?" She asked.

"The news reports only said that the boy fell in the tank and that you jumped in to save him. They didn't say how you managed to pull him from the mouth of a hungry Great White shark."

Jocelyne sighed. Her loose teal hair hung over her eyes and she glanced at it irritably. Flicking it behind her ear, she recounted the story. "I really don't know what happened. I saw him slip and fall in, I saw the shark grab him, and then I just dove in the water without thinking."

Mr. Otto nodded. "And what did you notice once you were in the water?"

"It was strange," Jocelyne said, "I didn't really think about it until after it was over. When I was in the tank, I was swimming really fast. Like, I don't even know how to describe it." She clamped her eyes shut tight as she tried to think. She could never forget that day, that terrible day as she watched the shark tear her brother's leg off in its teeth, but she remembered the feelings of the incident more than the actual events themselves. "It was like the water accepted me. Like I belonged there. And I could see," she remembered, "before that day, every time I opened my eyes underwater everything looked blurry. But that day, in the tank, it was all clear."

"Hm, I see." Mr. Otto muttered. "Anything else?"

She took a deep sigh. "There was one other thing," she said at last. "At one point, the shark let go of my brother and tried to attack me. When it did, I screamed. And then something happened."

"Something like what?"

"My scream was like a loud, shrill shriek. I've never screamed like that before or since. And I've never heard anything like it either. I made the shark stop. Then it just swam away like it didn't care anymore."

The older man adjusted his glasses. "I see. That's what I needed to know." The latches on the briefcase clicked as he unlocked it and lifted it open. "Well then, let's start from the very beginning. Your name."

"My name?" Jocelyne asked.

"Yes. Specifically, your last name. It isn't Chambers," Mr. Otto said. He pulled a sheet of paper from the briefcase and slid it across the table to her. It was a Birth Certificate. "Your name is McNeal. Jocelyne McNeal."

She took the certificate and looked over it. The first thing she noticed was that it wasn't issued in the United States, but from Scotland. She kept reading and found her first name listed on it, along with her birthday, and it indeed listed her last name as McNeal.

The next thing was the spot for her mother and father's names. Neither where those of the people she lived with. Instead, in the place for mother is listed someone named Clarisse McNeal. And the father's name was Connor.

She stared at the names for a long while, unsure of how to feel. "Is this me? These are my parents?" Her heart was racing, her mind was racing. "How did you get this?"

"From the records office in Scotland. And I have a confession to make. I'm not really a school counselor."

"You're not?"

"No." Mr. Otto slipped the birth certificate back in his

briefcase. "You could say I'm something of a private investigator. I've been hired by your real parents to find you and bring you home."

"My real parents?" Those words struck her harder now that she said them out loud. Those names on the birth certificate, Clarisse and Connor, they were her real parents and they were looking for her.

Mr. Otto continued. "But I can't take you back yet. Not until you've achieved your first change."

Jocelyne snapped back. "First change?"

"You have a heritage uniquely your own which you have barely begun to discover. I'm sure you've noticed."

"Noticed what?" Jocelyne asked.

"That day at the aquarium was the start of something amazing. It was your awakening. The way you swam and the way you cried out for help without knowing, all instinctive. And let me guess," he gestured to her hair. "That streak isn't dyed, is it?"

Jocelyne twirled the loose strands around her fingers. "No. Everyone thinks it is, but it's natural."

"And it didn't appear until after the incident, did it?"

"It did," Jocelyne confirmed.

Mr. Otto nodded, the hint of a smile on his face. "That blue-green streak in your hair is a physical expression of your unusual heritage. Your magical heritage. Your ocean heritage."

"My what?" Jocelyne stammered. "Magical? Like, what, are you saying I'm some kind of witch or something?" She rolled her eyes, folded her arms and leaned back in her chair. "Any of my old teachers could've told you that."

"Not a witch," Mr. Otto said. "Your magic has a connection with the ocean. You awakened it all the way back when you rescued your little brother from that shark in the aquarium, but it's been dormant ever since because your parental guardians have been purposefully holding you back."

Jocelyne felt she had enough. She stood up and held her hands out before her. "Okay, your dropping a lot on me all at once. I mean, secret parents, secret ocean powers, secret magic, it all seems a little nuts."

"I know it's a lot to take in," Mr. Otto said. He reached into the briefcase again and produced a glossy photograph. "If your parental figures had been raising you right, you would've learned all this years ago. Here, take this," he held the photo out to her.

Skeptically, Jocelyne grabbed the picture. It featured a man and woman on their wedding day, or at least she assumed it was their wedding as the woman wore a long white dress with a veil and held a bouquet of flowers, and the man wore a nice black tux. The woman's hair was dark brown with a streak of teal in the same place as Jocelyne's hair, while the man had sandy blonde hair.

Her eyes grew wide as she stared at the picture. "Is this . . ." she had a hard time forming the words, "my mom and dad?"

Mr. Otto nodded. "They want to meet you, but they can't until you fully awaken your gifts." He closed the briefcase and latched it. "I'll let you think about it for a day. You can keep that picture if you'd like, your parents would want you to have it." He stood and headed for the exit. "Contact me tomorrow with your decision. If I don't hear from you, I'll assume you don't want to continue and I won't bother you again." Without another word, he walked out of the food court and left Jocelyne alone with her thoughts and the photograph.

She stood that way for a long time, standing in the middle of the food court with the picture in hand, until at last she slipped the photo into the pocket of her jacket. She left the mall, finding her bike just how she left it. The ride back home seemed shorter than before, with her pulling into the backyard and locking her chain around the back porch almost without realizing it. She then climbed through her bedroom window just as someone knocked at her door.

"Jocelyne?" Shannon Chamber's voice came from the hallway.

"What?" Jocelyne called back, a little rushed and short of breath from biking.

"You've been in there for a while, I wanted to know if you were ready for lunch." Shannon's voice continued.

"Sure thing, Mom," Jocelyne kicked her shoes off and tucked them under her bed, and then tossed her jacket on the bed. "Just give me a minute."

"Are you alright?" the woman asked from behind the door, "you sound winded."

"I'm fine. Really." She said, trying not to breath so heavily.

"Well, I'm going to get your brothers and see if they're hungry. Come out when you're ready."

Shannon's footsteps faded down the hall as she walked away. Jocelyne heard the muffled sounds of her voice, along with those of Travis and Jacob coming from their room. She was hungry in truth, that small bowl of cereal hadn't been much compared to the eggs and bacon everyone else got, and it had been at least a couple hours since then, but she didn't want to face the woman right now.

She threw herself on the bed, wrapping her arms around the pillow and burying her face in it. She didn't know what she felt, hollow was probably a good word. She felt hollow inside, like there was an empty expanse in her chest where her heart should be.

She pulled the photograph from her jacket pocket, and stared at it again. The people in the picture, the man and woman, who were they really? According to Mr. Otto, the man was named Connor and the woman was named Clarisse. Her real parents, on the other side of the world, looking for her. But if so, why would they give her up in the first place? How much of what he said could she trust? And as for the people she lived with now, Benjamin and Shannon Chambers, how did they factor into this?

She remembered something then. It had nothing to do with her conversation with Mr. Otto or with what she overheard last night, but instead with something she saw every time they moved. During each move, the workers would carry a large trunk down from the attic. She remembered the first time she saw it, an old trunk that appeared to be covered in faded dingy leather with iron braces around it. She remembered distinctly that it had a big, metal, padlock on the front.

"Mommy, what's in that?" She remembered asking Shannon years ago during that move.

"Oh," Shannon seemed to be avoiding the question, "that's a secret thing for Mommy and Daddy." She said.

"What's in it?" Jocelyne pressed.

"Nothing you need to worry about. One day I'll show you." Shannon had stroked Jocelyne's hair and given her a small kiss on the forehead. This was about the time her streak was starting to appear in her hair.

That was the last time they spoke of the object in the attic. So why did she remember it now? *It's a secret,* Shannon had said, *One day I'll show you.*

Jocelyne sat up and set the photo down on her bedside table beside her radio alarm clock. She turned the radio off. Today would be that day. She walked across her room, strolled out into the hall, and marched down to her brothers' room. Shannon had left since then, probably back to prepare lunch, meaning the only two in the room itself where the boys, Travis and Jacob. She twisted the knob and pushed the door open without knocking, finding Travis on the computer playing some swords and sorcery adventure game with a big set of headphones over his ears, and Jacob lying on the top bunk of their bed reading a book.

Jacob glanced over at her, briefly annoyed, and then returned to the book. "What, Jocy?"

Jocelyne let out a heavy sigh, then folded her arms and leaned against the door frame. "I need your help."

Chapter Five

Jacob turned away from his book and looked at Jocelyne with his eyebrow arched. "I'm sorry, what was that?"

"I said I need your help." She repeated.

Jacob smirked. He sat up and set the book aside. Jocelyne hated that smirk. It was his "I'll help you for a price" smirk. The one he wore whenever he thought he could get something out of a deal.

Jacob tossed the pillow at the back of Travis's head. It hit his brother with a soft flump, who turned around and slipped the headphones off. "What is it?" Travis asked smartly.

"Big sis wants a favor of us." Jacob explained, then turned

his attention back to Jocelyne. "So, what kind of help are we talking about?"

"There's an old trunk in the attic." Jocelyne said. "It has a padlock on it. I need to get the key out of Mom and Dad's room so I can open it."

Travis swiveled around in his chair. "What's in it?"

Jocelyne shrugged. "I don't know. That's why I want to see." It wasn't a total lie, not really. She truly did not know what the twin's parents kept hidden away in that trunk, but she figured it had something to do with her true parents and who Jocelyne really was. "I want to know what dirty secrets Mom and Dad have up there."

Jacob swung his legs over the edge of his bunk and kicked them back and forth. "What do you want us to do?" He leaned back on both arms and cocked his head to one side, still smirking.

"I need to get into their bedroom to find the key. I know they keep it hidden somewhere. I just don't know where exactly." Jocelyne said.

"Hm," Travis pulled open his computer drawer and reached in. "You mean this key?" He held up a small, iron key. It was an old style, the kind that came from the eighteen hundreds or earlier, with a metal hoop at the end tied with a piece of red yarn.

Jocelyne's eyes snapped wide. "How did you get that?"

"I found it." Travis said coyly. "When going through their things. Did you know their sock drawer has a false bottom? That's where I found this thing."

"Well, give it." Jocelyne strutted over to him and held out her hand. "I need that."

As she approached, Travis tossed the key to his brother still on the top of the bunk beds. "We will," Jacob slipped it under the blankets and pulled his legs up. He rested his elbows on his knees and placed the tips of his fingers together, trying to make himself look devious and sinister. Jocelyne just thought it made him look ridiculous. "But you have to do something for us."

Jocelyne sighed and rolled her eyes. Here it comes, the crazy demands of a pair of eleven-year-old boys just to get one little thing. Instinctively, she blew the loose strand of hair away from her face. "What do you want?"

"Well," Jacob drew the word out, making Jocelyne wait, and then said, "we wanna see that new movie."

"Which one?" Jocelyne asked, her annoyance growing.

"Nature Trail of Death!" Travis shouted, both his arms thrust over his head.

Jocelyne stared at them both with her mouth hung open and eyes blank. "What?" She said in a flat tone. "Really?"

"Yeah!" Jacob confirmed with just as much enthusiasm as his brother. "It just came out! Nature Trail of Death! In 3-D!"

Jocelyne pinched the bridge of her nose, her eyes shut tight. "You can't be serious."

"Oh, yes we are!" Jacob smiled. "It's about a psycho killer who hunts down and kills a troop of boy scouts out in the woods with an axe!"

"How do you know that? Have you seen it already?" Jocelyne asked.

"No, it just came out. As we just said." Travis smacked his hand against this forehead. "Duh!"

"Then how do you know so much about it?"

"They've had trailers all over the internet for months! We've been dying to see it, but Mom and Dad won't take us," Jacob said. "They say we're too young to see R-rated movies."

"That's because you are." Jocelyne said. "Besides, how would I even get you in to see the movie if it's rated R?"

"That's what you need to figure out." Travis smirked and leaned back in his computer chair. "Take us to the movie, and we'll give you the key."

Jocelyne folded her arms. "Give me the key first, and I'll consider it."

"No considering." Jacob laid himself down on the blanket to keep the key covered. "Promise to take us, or we'll put it back where we found it."

"Give it to me, or I'll tell Mom and Dad you were snooping around in their room." Jocelyne retorted.

"You tell Mom and Dad, and we'll tell them you snuck out this morning." Travis smirked.

"What?" Jocelyne blinked. "What do you . . . How do you . . ." She scowled and clenched her fists. "You little brats were sneaking into my room again, weren't you?!"

"It's not sneaking. You left your door unlocked." Travis said.

"You still shouldn't have been in there!" Jocelyne snapped. "That's MY room, not yours!"

"So what? We still have the key." Jacob pulled it out and dangled it from the piece of red twine. "Movie, then key." He proposed.

"Key, then movie." Jocelyne argued back and crossed her arms again. "No other deal."

They stared at one another for a long time. The key slowly swung back and forth on its string. After a long while, Jacob flicked it up and caught it. "Alright, fine." He said, and tossed it to her.

Jocelyne, caught off guard, blinked for a second and tried to grab the key. She missed and it clinked to the floor. She snatched it up. "Thank you," she said with a hint of sarcasm.

"How long do you think? A week?" Jacob said as he turned to his brother.

"Yeah, a week." Travis nodded, then faced Jocelyne again. "You have one week to get us to the movie. If you haven't taken us by then, we'll tell on you."

"Ugh," Jocelyne rolled her eyes. "Alright, fine," she scoffed, and turned to leave.

Just as she stepped out the door, she crashed into something. "Oof!" Jocelyne stumbled back, her fingers clenched tight around the key, and looked up to see the woman standing in the hallway.

"Jocelyne," Shannon Chambers said in startlement, "sorry, I didn't see you. Are you alright?" The woman placed her hands on Jocelyne's shoulders as if to steady her.

"Yes, Mom, I'm fine," Jocelyne stuffed the hand holding the key into her pocket. "What's going on?"

"I just came to tell you lunch was ready. I have some tuna

sandwiches in the kitchen." Shannon said.

"I love tuna!" Jacob rolled off the top bunk and jumped to the floor. "Just as long as it doesn't have any relish in it, I hate that stuff."

"Me, too." Travis stood from his computer desk.

Jocelyne liked tuna, too. More than any other kind of sandwich, actually. Now that she thought of it, if what Mr. Otto said was true about ocean magic and a secret heritage, that made a lot more sense now.

They ate lunch at the dining room table. It consisted of the tuna fish sandwich, a glass of lemonade, and a few apple slices. No one talked much. Shannon asked what the boy's had planned for their first day of summer vacation, and they answered with simple declarations of "Not much."

After lunch, Jocelyne went back to her room to wait. She lay on the bed with her hands behind her head, staring up at the ceiling. The old, iron key rested heavily in her pocket. She thought about the talk with Mr. Otto and all the things he said. How he told her that her mother wanting to meet her, but not until after her first change. What was that supposed to mean? What was the first change?

Maybe the trunk in the attic could give some answers. Even

so, Jocelyne thought she might have an idea. It had to do with what she remembered about the aquarium incident. How well she could swim and how long she held her breath, the fact that they always lived along the coast even though she wasn't allowed to swim in the ocean, and her scream that pacified the shark.

What had Mr. Otto called it? Her magical ocean heritage? That really only brought one idea to mind, and it sounded ridiculous even in her own thoughts. Was she, maybe . . .

No, that was silly. Absolutely stupid. Something a five-year-old would say. There was no way she could be a–

"Mermaid," she said the word and almost immediately started laughing. It sounded even more crazy out loud, but it seemed to fit. So stupid, so insane, but strangely reasonable.

She stayed in her room, reading the rest of the day. She only came out again later that evening when Benjamin came home.

"Jocelyne, boys, would you come out to the front room for a minute, please," their father's voice rang from down the hall.

Jocelyne slipped a bookmark between the pages and set the book on her nightstand beside her cell phone. She came out to meet her fake parents and took her spot on the couch beside the twins. Ben and Shannon stood side-by-side in the center of the room, facing the three of them.

"Kids, we have a few things to announce," Shannon said, her face was beaming with joy.

"Are you pregnant?" Travis blurted, cutting them off before the adults could continue.

"Is it a girl? Are we going to have a baby sister?" Jacob interjected. "I want a new sister, this one is defective." He jabbed a thumb at Jocelyne.

"I'd just like some new siblings in general." Jocelyne turned to glare at them. "Can we return these ones? I think they're broken."

"All right, cut it out. All of you." Ben snapped. The kids fell back on the couch, silent. Jocelyne braced her head on her hand as she leaned against the armrest. "You're mother's not pregnant, and no one is getting a baby sister."

"What's really happening," Shannon clasped her hands together and smiled, "is we're going on a big family vacation together!"

Jocelyne shifted in her seat. "Vacation?" She asked. "I thought I was grounded."

"Your mother and I talked it over, and we decided that maybe a whole month was too harsh." Ben said. "In light of this new decision, you are ungrounded."

"Where are we going?" Jacob asked, suddenly interested. He leaned forward.

"We've decided," Ben said as he looked over at Shannon. They seemed to flash each other knowing glances. "We're going to Scotland!"

"Scotland?" Jocelyne almost jumped off the couch.

"Yes," Shannon exclaimed. "That's where I was born."

"We'll need to get you kids some passports." Ben said. "And once they come in, we'll set a date. How does that sound?"

"Sounds pretty cool, Dad." Travis stated, followed by an agreeing "Yeah," from Jacob.

"Good." Ben nodded, not noticing or not caring that Jocelyne hadn't said anything. "And as for tonight, how would you kids like to go out for pizza?"

"Awesome!" Jacob and Travis shouted in near unison.

"Then go get your shoes." Ben said.

The boys were both off the couch and running for the hall closet almost before Ben said anything. Jocelyne stayed on the couch for a few minutes longer. They'd never taken any family vacations like this before, and certainly never to another country. Why were they doing this all of a sudden?

"Jocy?" Shannon came to sit beside her and placed a hand on the young girl's shoulder. "You feeling alright?"

"Huh?" She pulled away and stood. "Yeah, Mom, I'm fine." She followed the boys to the closet and grabbed her shoes.

Chapter Six

That night, she lay in bed until it was fully dark. The digital readout on her alarm clock glowed with a bright green light. Jocelyne stared at it and watched as the numbers changed slowly and the night wore on. Finally, when the numbers shifted from 11:59 pm to 12:00 am, she pushed the blankets off and got to her feet. Clasped in her hands, she held the heavy iron key.

Dressed in her seashell pajamas, Jocelyne moved on tiptoes from her room into the empty hallway. Without the light from her alarm clock, it was darker out here than in her room, the hallway seemed to stretch away, and disappear into blackness. She placed her hand on the wall to steady herself, and walked quietly in the direction of her parents' room. Her bare feet pressed soundlessly into the soft carpet with each step.

Ahead of her was another open door with a pillar of blue fluorescent light spilling out. The light came from her parent's alarm clock, and in this darkness it stung her eyes. As she approached, she stopped. Jocelyne didn't want to get caught out of bed, She came up beside the door, pressed her back to the wall, and listened.

She heard Ben's snoring, and sighed with relief. Both asleep. Good. Try to keep it that way. Jocelyne slipped past their bedroom and continued down the hall. Once she passed her parents' room, she took her cell phone from the pocket of her pajamas and turned on the flashlight. Its unnatural white light flooded the hall.

At the very end of the corridor was the attic hatch, a square door in the ceiling that opened into a ladder. A rope dangled from one end of the hatch. Jocelyne gripped the rope and tugged it lightly. At first, nothing happened and the door remained closed. She pulled on it again, a little harder this time, and each time she did the hatch loosened just a bit until at last the door fell open and the ladder unfolded.

She caught the bottom rung of the ladder just as it came

towards her. She set it down gently on the carpet, doing her best not to make noise, and started to climb.

The attic was musty, dusty, and dark. Holding up her phone light, she saw piles of cardboard boxes stacked all the way to the slanted wood planks and supports of the roof. Most had big letters scrawled across them in black ink, things like winter clothes or spare blankets, but Jocelyne wasn't interested in any of that. She wanted the chest.

She crawled inside. The attic floor creaked under her hands and feet, and Jocelyne winced. Lifting her foot, the wood groaned and she resettled her weight. Each step brought another quiet creak from the attic floor. She bit her lip and stood up, wincing just a little and the wood emitted little noises. She had to be quick if she didn't want to wake the rest of the house.

Jocelyne held her phone out before her as she moved through the maze of boxes, looking up and down the rows for the chest or trunk, something that looked like it could take the iron key in her hand. As she scanned the light over a pile of boxes, something caught her eye and she turned back to shine the light over it again. It was a great, black trunk, made of wood with metal bindings and covered in a leather coating. A heavy padlock looped through the rungs on the front.

A stack of cardboard boxes rested on top of the chest. Jocelyne slipped the key back into her pocket and set her phone on the floor so its light was facing upward, then got to work pulling the boxes off and setting them aside. The first box was heavier than she expected and she almost fell backwards when she pulled it down. She strained, holding her breath, and then placed it on the floor beside her. She did the same for the rest of the boxes until the chest was completely uncovered. Then she knelt in front of it, and retrieved the key from her pocket.

She looked at it for a moment, holding it in the light of her phone and twirling it in her fingers. She slipped the key into the hole in the padlock and turned it. There was a metallic click and the lock popped open.

Just then, the open hatchway was flooded with yellow light as the hall light turned on. Jocelyne snapped her head around, her hair whipping at her face as her breath caught and heart rate jumped. She grabbed her phone and shut off the flashlight before crouching behind the boxes.

"What the . . ." Ben Chamber's voice rose up from the hallway below. "Must not have been secured very well." There was a creaking of hinges as the ladder was folded up and the attic door pushed back in place. Jocelyne heard a click from the other side of the hatch as it was locked. The yellow light from the hall shut off and she could hear her father walking back to his room. Trapped. She was locked in the attic.

Jocelyne sat up and turned on her phone light again. She shined it on the pad lock, which hung open on the chest loop. She pulled the lock off, set it beside her, unhooked the pair of latches, and lifted the lid. Its rusty hinges squeaked and groaned in protest. Taking her phone again, he brought it over the inside of the trunk and gazed at its contents.

She didn't know what to expect, but what she found confused her. This big trunk held only two items. The first appeared to be a fur coat, neatly folded and tucked in one side of the chest. It was light brown and covered with black speckles. Jocelyne brushed her fingers lightly over it and was amazed at how soft it was. Why would Ben and Shannon keep a fur coat in the attic?

The other item looked duller, but piqued her interest more. A photo album. It was off white with imprinted letters of imitation gold that read, *Our Memories*. There was a picture on the front of the book that showed the same man and woman as in the photo Mr. Otto had given her. They were even dressed the same, in their wedding outfits. Jocelyne lifted the album out of the trunk. She blew a fine layer of dust off its cover, then opened it.

Holding her phone light over the pages, she scanned her eyes over the pictures and their captions with awed amazement. The same man and woman stood side by side, her dressed in a long white gown with a handful of flowers, and him in a nice black tuxedo. They were laughing and smiling, smearing wedding cake on each other's faces. The pictures were all labeled with Connor and Clarisse McNeal.

Her phone beeped at her, alerting that the battery was running low. She closed the photo album and set it on the floor beside her, then shut the lid of the trunk, hooked the lock through the hoops, and closed it. She stood, tucked the photo album under her arm, and looked around.

The attic was dark again, with just a little light from the outside street lights coming through the circular front window. Now, as she spun in a circle, the question came up again. How was she to get out of here?

Chapter Seven

The attic door was locked. That fact, plain as day, kept coming back to her. She couldn't go out the same way she came. She'd have to figure out some other way. Jocelyne turned around in a circle again and again, looking all around the attic for another way out.

All she saw were the dark shapes of boxes stacked atop one another and the slanted support beams of the roof. Maybe if she had some more light she could see things better, but her phone was almost dead. Without it, the only light in the attic came from the street lamp outside through the small, round window.

She froze in place, then smacked her hand against her forehead. Of course, duh! Readjusting the photo album under her arm, she maneuvered her way through the maze of boxes over to the window. When she got to it, Jocelyne ran her free hand around the edges of the glass, feeling for a seam or depression of some kind. Something to signify that the window could be opened. She found nothing.

Jocelyne let out a tired breath. Of course it wouldn't open. She leaned forward and pressed her head against the glass. It shifted a little. She blinked and pulled back. Delicately, she placed her fingers against the window pane and pushed. The glass shifted again.

The window was made of four separate sheets of glass held in place by a wooden frame in the shape of a giant plus sign. The years of sun and rain had warped the wood so the glass didn't fit as snug as it used to. Setting the album on the floor, Jocelyne placed both her hands against one corner of the window and pushed up. The glass shifted up and popped out of its frame. A little laugh rose from her chest. Jocelyne kept one hand pressed firm against the loose glass and carefully, so as not to cut herself, grabbed it by the corner with her other hand and pulled the window pane out of the frame. She then did the same for the other four sections of the window.

She had to break the frame itself. She placed the palm of her hand on the cross in the middle and gave it one hard shove. The wood snapped almost without effort. With that done, Jocelyne set the photo album out on the roof overlooking the porch. She then crawled on her hands and knees out through the round hole.

The roof sloped downward under her feet. She tried to stand, and almost lost her balance. Her arms whirled around as she teetered back and forth, and she quickly sat back down. Standing was out of the question. The rough grains of the roof shingles dug into her palms and the bottoms of her feet.

She scooted along until she could look over the edge. The ground was still ten feet, maybe closer to fifteen, from where she sat. She might be able to jump, but it looked so far down. And what if she got hurt? She remembered when she used to climb trees and jump down, the way her legs would tingle after hitting the ground. Those were much shorter drops, what would this one be like? What if she sprained her ankle, or even broke her leg?

She could imagine herself splayed out on the front lawn with the lower half of one leg bent in the wrong direction, crying and screaming at the top of her lungs. That would awaken the adults in the house, who would then take her to the hospital where she would stay for weeks with her leg in a cast. And then all the questions that would come after. What were you doing on the roof? How did this window get broken? Why were you sneaking around? How did you get that photo album? No jumping, then.

Jocelyne tucked the album under her arm again and crawled across the roof to where it jutted out over the house. The gutter ran along the edge of the roof until it came to the corner, held up by a support beam. She tossed the album to the ground where it landed with a soft thud, and then steeled herself for the next part. She would need to shimmy down the storm gutter support to the ground.

She turned around and dangled one leg over the ledge of the roof. Supporting herself on just her arms, she brought her other leg over the edge and hooked them around the support beam. She glanced over her shoulder, then turned away as a sudden rush of vertigo swept over her. Jocelyne took several deep breaths, trying to slow her racing heart. Keeping her legs wrapped tightly around the gutter support, she lowered herself first to her elbows, and then just her fingertips. Slowly, she let go of the gutter, one hand at a time, and wrapped both of her arms around the beam.

She slid down the porch support, clinging to it like a frightened child, until one foot touched the cold, dew-covered grass beneath her. She gasped in delight, released her death grip, and stood. Her heart still raced, and a film of nervous sweat coated her skin, but she had made it. Picking up the photo album again, Jocelyne walked around the side of the house to her bedroom window. She tossed the album in, then pulled herself over the window sill and landed softly on her bed.

She knew the smart thing to do was to sleep, to crawl under the covers, close her eyes, and let herself drift off, but she was too anxious now. She only got a brief moment to thumb through the pictures in the album before her phone started to die on her, now she wanted to look at them more closely. She clicked on her bedside light, pulled herself up so she sat cross-legged on her bed, pulled the photo album into her lap, and opened it again.

Her real mom and dad. She placed her hand across the photos, as if touching made it more real. As she flipped through the pages, she moved away from the wedding day to other snapshots, such as the honeymoon. There were pictures of them standing at the edge of a cliff overlooking the ocean, beautiful green fields and hills crisscrossed with streams. Was this her home?

Among those in the pictures she also saw her parents. She caught herself with that thought, and shook her head to dislodge it. Not her parents, just the people who'd kept her all these years.

Ben and Shannon Chambers. They were standing beside the other couple in some of the pictures, the two women sometimes hugged each other. So they knew her true parents, after all.

Turning the pages and looking deeper into the album, Jocelyne found pictures of the woman, her real mother, with a hand resting over her pregnant belly. Pregnant with her.

The last picture in the book showed her mother, Clarisse, in a hospital bed, clearly exhausted, with messy hair and puffy cheeks. She had one of those little finger clamps on to monitor her pulse. Shannon and Ben Chambers stood on one side of the bed, and her father, Connor, stood on the other side. A tiny bundle lay cradled in Clarisse's arms, the small still face of a sleeping newborn wrapped up in a blanket. Jocelyne found her eyes drawn to the message scrawled on the page just beneath this last picture.

Happy Birthday, Jocelyne!

She found herself tearing up. At first she didn't notice, until a drop splashed on the page. She sniffled and wiped her eyes before closing the book. Jocelyne clicked off her bedside lamp, then curled under the blankets with her arm draped over the photo album. She ran her fingers across the imprinted letters, Our Memories. Yes, indeed, this held the memories she wanted.

Her real family. She fell asleep that way.

Jocelyne dreamed of the ocean that night. She saw the choppy waves, crested with yellow-white foam. Beneath the surface, schools of fish darted together in quick flashes. She swam with a grace she had never known, as though the water was her home, calling to her.

Chapter Eight

"You found this in a trunk in your attic?" Mr. Otto asked. Jocelyne pressed her phone close against her ear. The early morning light fell through the window to land across the open photo album she held on her lap.

"Yeah," she whispered into the phone. She tried not to speak too loud, she didn't want anyone to hear. Upon waking this morning, the first thing she did was plug in her phone to charge, and then called Mr. Otto. His voice was scratchy at first, clearly she'd woken him up. Jocelyne turned the page and came upon the picture of her mother in the hospital again. "I remembered the trunk always moving with us, and never being told what was in it. So I decided to check for myself."

"Did you find anything else in the trunk?" Mr. Otto asked.

"A fur coat, I think." Jocelyne closed the album and set it aside. "It felt like a fur coat."

"And did you feel anything when you saw it? Or touched it?"

Jocelyne shrugged. "It felt soft, I guess. Nothing else."

"Alright." Mr. Otto's voice came over the cell phone's speaker. "So I take it you want to know more?"

"Yes." Jocelyne said and nodded. "Absolutely."

"Good. Then I would like to meet you today at the Recreation Center this afternoon if you can." Mr. Otto said. "I will have something for you when you get there, and I will be able to explain more."

"What time?"

"Let's say 2:30. That should give me enough time."

"Okay." Jocelyne said. "I'll see you then." She pressed the disconnect button and set the phone on her bedside table to finish charging.

It was Saturday, not that it made much of a difference to her now that school was out, but that did mean Ben wouldn't be leaving for work today. At least being ungrounded meant she didn't have to worry about sneaking out of the house again.

She checked the readout on her phone. It was 10:30 in the morning. Four hours until she was supposed to meet with Mr. Otto at the Rec center. What to do until then?

She closed the photo album and slipped it under her bed. There was no way she was going to hide it back in the attic, not now that she had it. It was hers, after all. It held her only connection to her real parents, and she wasn't going to let that go. Besides, it was hard enough getting it out of the attic, no reason to break her neck putting it back.

She got out of bed and made her way to the kitchen for breakfast. She opened the freezer and pulled out a box of frozen waffles. No cold cereal for her today. Sure, it wasn't the yummy breakfast of eggs and bacon that everyone else had yesterday, but it was still better than plain cheerios.

She'd just put the waffles in the toaster and pushed the lever down when Ben Chambers came into the kitchen. "Good morning, Jocelyne," he said.

"Morning." She only gave a cursory glance as she waited for the toaster.

"Do you have any big plans for the day?" Ben put a white filter and a bag of french roast in the instant coffee maker.

The toaster popped. Jocelyne snatched the warm waffles and

set them on a plate before gathering the butter, syrup, and milk from the fridge. "I thought I'd meet up with some friends today." She lied.

"Oh, really? Where are you guys going?" He was probing. Trying to find if she had any hidden plans.

"Don't know yet." Jocelyne said. "We'll probably figure it out later."

"What are their names?" Ben asked.

Jocelyne froze, a knife in hand with butter half-spread across the top waffle. She blinked once, and then twice, her brain running a million miles a minute as she desperately tried to think up some name. Nothing came up. "Geez, Dad," she finally blurted, "do you have to know every moment of my life?"

"There's no need to raise your voice," Ben poured hot coffee into a mug. "I just want to make sure you're alright."

"Well, I'm fine." She said, squeezing the bottle of maple syrup all over the waffles. She filled a cup with milk, then took her breakfast to the table and scarfed it down. Before Ben could join her, she'd finished eating, rinsed her plate and cup, and set them in the dishwasher.

"Jocelyne," he called to her as she started for her room.

"What now?" Her voice full of irritation.

"I want you to know I love you, baby girl."

Jocelyne hadn't expected that. She found herself standing at the edge of the hallway with her hand placed against the wall, unsure of what to say or how to feel. "Yeah," she said at last, "you, too." She then continued back to her room.

She lay on her bed and read for the next few hours. Her radio blared nearby, drowning out all other sounds or thoughts. At long last, when it was almost two in the afternoon, she slipped the bookmark back between the pages, and set the book aside. She passed by her brothers' room on the way out, neither really noticed her, and the adults in the living room watching TV. "You going out to meet your friends?" Ben asked.

"Yes," she slipped on her shoes by the door.

"Well, have fun. Tell us how it goes." Shannon said and waved as Jocelyne stepped outside.

"Sure," Jocelyne gave little response. She was out the door and, before even realizing it, on her bike and pedaling down the street.

Why were they acting so nice today? Did they suspect something? Had they seen the broken window to the attic? Did they overhear her phone call this morning? She tried to be quiet, but maybe not quiet enough.

She arrived at the Recreation center and found only one car in the parking lot, a red Ford Focus. She propped her bicycle beside the bike rack and chained it in place, then went inside. She spotted Mr. Otto seated at a small table in the front lobby, a picture book laid out before him. "Hi," she said.

"Hello." Mr. Otto stood up and waved. He wore a red polo shirt and a pair of khaki shorts today with Velcro sandals. "Glad you could make it. Come over, have a seat."

Jocelyne did as she was asked. She took the chair across from Mr. Otto and placed her hands on the table. "What are you reading?" She asked, referring to the picture book.

Mr. Otto closed the book and rested his hand over the cover. "I'll get to that in a minute. Now, let's get to the point. Ms. Jocelyne," he said as he adjusted his glasses, "you want to know the truth, don't you"

"Yes," She said and nodded without hesitation. "Everything."

"Alright. Let's go back to what I said yesterday. You remember what I told you about your ocean heritage." Mr. Otto laced his fingers together.

"My magical ocean heritage." Jocelyne said. "Yes, I remember."

"Have you given any thought to what I meant?"

Jocelyne averted her eyes. The back of her neck felt hot and a weird prickly sensation moved up her arms. "A little." She said. "I think you implied I'm not entirely human." The words were low, almost mumbled.

Mr. Otto nodded. "So far, so good. Anything else?"

"And that I'm really some fantastical water creature." Jocelyne continued, more confidence in her tone.

"Getting warmer." Mr. Otto said. "Do you have any idea what you might be?"

Her heart raced. She stared down at the table as her hands clenched into fists. She couldn't remember the last time she felt this nervous. "Maybe," she didn't want to be wrong, "I'm a . . ." She stopped, still unable to say the thought out loud.

"Mermaid?" Mr. Otto finished her statement for her.

Her head snapped up and eyes grew wide. "How did you . . ?"

"Many young ladies first think that when they are introduced to the idea. At least, those that grew up on the outside." He leaned back in the chair and pushed the book forward. "However, that is not the case."

"It's not?" Jocelyne said, her voice full of disappointment.

"Sorry, you're not a mermaid." He said. "Don't feel so bad.

Mermaids aren't all they're cracked up to be. Kinda snobbish, full of themselves, stuck up and rude to everyone not a mermaid. Imagine elves with fins and you've got a good idea what merfolk are like. And I mean the High elves, not the ones that make cookies. Those ones are alright."

Jocelyne didn't quite know what to feel. She slumped back in the chair, her hand slid off the table and fell in her lap. "So then, what am I?" Jocelyne asked.

"Collectively, all the people of the ocean, all with a magical water heritage, are known as Water Denizens." Mr. Otto explained. "This does include mermaids, as well as every other ocean fae, water spirit, changeling, gill man, and deep one. It's a massive underwater society."

"Which one am I?" Jocelyne asked with growing impatience.

Mr. Otto smiled. "A selkie."

"Huh?" Jocelyne blinked in confusion. She'd never heard that term before. "A what?"

The old man leaned in close, raised an eyebrow and smirked. "You're a selkie, Jocy."

Jocelyne blinked once, then twice. She sat still in the chair, glancing around the room before returning to Mr. Otto's gaze. "I'm a what?"

The smirk and cocked eyebrow immediately fell off Mr. Otto's face. He let out a sigh and rubbed his eyes. "Yeah, I should've expected that." He pushed the picture book towards her again. "Here, read this real quick."

She scanned the front cover. It featured a woman in a black mourning dress with a look of forlorn longing, standing on a beach overlooking the sun setting into the ocean. A pair of seals floated in the water, looking back at the woman with a similar expression of sadness. The book's title, *The Selkie Bride*, scrawled across the cover in elegant cursive font.

Jocelyne opened the book and started to read. It was a simple picture book, intended for little kids, that told of a lonely fisherman who one day spotted a beautiful woman walking alone on the beach. He tried to call out to her, but as soon as he did, the woman grabbed a seal skin off a nearby rock and dove into the ocean. The fisherman saw a seal swim away from shore and came to realize the woman was a selkie, a seal woman.

"A SEAL!!?" Jocelyne's scream rang throughout the room. She jumped out of her chair and knocked the book to the floor. "You're telling me I'm a seal!?"

"A selkie," Mr. Otto corrected. "A seal person. A type of shapeshifter." He picked up the picture book and placed it back on the table. "Like most Water Denizens, you have both a human and an aquatic form that you can change into."

Jocelyne looked down at the cover of the book again. "And my aquatic form is a seal?" She took her seat again. "How can you be sure?"

"Because your mother is a selkie," Mr. Otto said. "And your father, while he isn't one, is descended from a selkie mother. With that kind of heritage, it's nearly impossible not to be."

She didn't quite know what to think, it all seemed too crazy. Seal parents, a secret society of water dwelling people. If she hadn't found the photo album in the attic, she probably wouldn't even be entertaining the idea.

"You look confused." Mr. Otto reached under his chair, lifted up his briefcase, and set it on the table. "I know. It's a lot to take in all at once. And you don't completely believe me. That's why I came prepared." He popped the briefcase open and pulled out two folded, foam wetsuits.

"What are these?" Jocelyne asked.

"These are Changeling Suits," Otto explained. "They're designed to shapeshift along with you. Normal clothes don't change when a Water Denizen takes on their aquatic form, so these were made to accommodate that."

Jocelyne looked from one to the other. They seemed like ordinary diving or scuba suits made of insulated foam rubber. One was obviously larger than the other, a charcoal color with patches and highlights of lighter gray and red. The other, smaller and child-sized, was also charcoal gray, but with highlights of teal running along the sides to the shoulders.

"This one's for you," Mr. Otto pushed the gray and teal one to Jocelyne. He grabbed the picture book and placed it back in the briefcase before closing it, then took the other wetsuit. "Now it's time to show you what I mean," he said as he stood.

"Show me?" Jocelyne asked.

"Of course. How do you think I know so much about all this?" Mr. Otto said. "I'm a Water Denizen, too." He headed out of the lobby, walking down the hall past a sign that pointed towards the indoor swimming pool.

Jocelyne placed her hands on the wetsuit, or rather the Changeling Suit as Otto had called it. She unfolded and held it out in front of her, examining it. The sleeves and legs were short, coming down to her elbows and knees at most, and a zipper ran up the back. She narrowed her eyes and twisted her lips in a critical look. With a sigh, she tucked the suit under her arm and followed Otto.

The pool room was immense, with a high ceiling and large open windows to let in sunlight. There were diving platforms along both short ends of the pool, and waiting benches lining the long sides. The water had a slight blue tinge to it and reached ten feet at its deepest point. Jocelyne found Mr. Otto just as he came out of the restroom, now dressed in the Changeling Suit, the sleeves and legs of which reached all the way to his wrists and ankles. "Okay, Ms. Jocelyne," he said as he did some pre-swimming stretches, "I'm going to show you what I mean."

"I hope it's good," Jocelyne muttered to herself. She sat on one of the benches, the teal wetsuit rested in her lap, and propped her elbows on her knees and her chin in her hands.

Mr. Otto stepped right to the edge of the swimming pool so his toes dangled over the lip, then he placed his hands together, bent his knees, and dove into the water.

Jocelyne watched as Mr. Otto swam. The ripples and waves from his splash distorted his image, but she thought she could see something happening. His head looked bigger than it used to, his body smaller, and his limbs appeared more fluid.

Otto circled back in the water and came towards the spot he jumped from. He dove deeper, disappearing from Jocelyne's view. Just as she stood up to get a closer look, a thick, slimy tentacle reached over the edge of the pool. It was followed by a second, and then a third. Then the bulbous, orange head of a huge octopus emerged from the water.

Jocelyne screamed, her voice echoed off the walls of the pool area. She bolted to her feet and tried to jump back, but her legs caught on the bench and she fell, sprawling to the floor.

The big, black eyes twisted to focus on her, and Jocelyne felt a shiver run up her spine. The tentacles seemed to reach for her. She scurried backwards, crawling on her hands and pushing away with her feet.

The arms pulled back and the octopus slid back into the pool. Jocelyne sat with her back pressed against a wall, her chest heaving for breath, and watched the water's edge. A hand, an ordinary human hand grabbed hold of the ledge and Mr. Otto climbed out of the pool.

"You're an OCTOPUS!?" Jocelyne shouted.

Otto grabbed a towel from the bench and started to dry off. "I am," he said. "Specifically, a Giant Pacific Octopus."

"Why are you an octopus!?"

Otto shrugged. "Genetics, I guess. Plus a little oceanic magic."

"It's weird," Jocelyne shuddered and stuck her tongue out.

"All slimy and boneless and tentacles and suckers. Blech! Gross!"

"That's specist," Mr. Otto draped the towel over his shoulders. "It's not as though I'm insulting you because you're a selkie. Kids these days are so rude."

"You could've at least warned me before shape shifting," Jocelyne said as she stood. She picked up the teal and gray wetsuit and clutched it close to her chest.

"But now you know it's all true," Otto stated. "Everything I've told you about your parents, your heritage, and your magical abilities. You've discovered most of it for yourself."

Jocelyne glanced down at the wetsuit in her arms. "So, what do I do from here?"

"Now, we need to work on your first transformation." Mr. Otto said. "For that, we're going to need to practice every day until you get it. You'd better get changed, we start today."

Chapter Nine

Otto paced around his hotel room, his hands clasped behind his back and his brow furled, deep in thought. His wetsuit hung in the shower to drip dry. Jocelyne's first change was taking longer than he wanted. It had been almost a week since the day at the Recreation center and the indoor swimming pool, and she had made no real advancement. Well, that wasn't completely true.

He paused and glanced up toward the ceiling. Her speed in the water and the length she could hold her breath had both spiked exponentially. Jocelyne was now faster than even the best Olympic swimmer and could stay under for nearly thirty minutes. On the second day of practice, she'd forgone goggles altogether, claiming she could see fine without them.

But despite all that, no seal skin formed, no matter how long she stayed in the water. Otto's concerns grew more with each passing day. She had the gift, he knew that much, the teal streaks in her hair was proof enough of that, and her improvements at swimming showed her latent ability, but it was the girl's upbringing that restricted her. If Jocelyne had been taught earlier, she would already have her skin and be a full fledged selkie.

The problem was the girl's guardians. They were holding her back, intentionally so. What Jocelyne really needed right now was another selkie. Otto could show her how he shifts from man to octopus a thousand times and it wouldn't help. But another selkie would be just the thing.

He fell back into the overstuffed easy chair and sighed. With no other selkie, at least none that he knew of, they would need something else. Otto placed a hand across his chin as he thought. Jocelyne had only ever accessed her latent abilities once, and that was as a child in the aquarium with the shark. Of course, throwing her in a tank with a hungry Great White was out of the question, it was too dangerous. Plus, no one kept Great Whites in captivity anymore, not after that incident with Jocelyne and her brothers.

But, maybe, there was another way.

He checked his watch.7:45 in the evening. Good, still early enough to make the call. He snatched his phone off the bedside table, dialed the number, and placed it to his ear. It rang three times before a voice came over the other line.

"Aloha," it said.

"Aloha, Shawn," he replied, "this is Mr. Otto."

"Hey, what's up, Doc Ock? Haven't heard from you in a while," The young man said. "You still traveling?"

"I'm in California, actually, working on a case. That's the reason I called." He leaned back in his chair and crossed his legs. "How soon would you be able to fly out here if I asked?"

"Oh, I don't know," Shawn said with some hesitation. "It's not exactly a short flight. Why do you need me?"

"It's the case I mentioned. I'm working with this girl, trying to help her with the first shift, and it's not going so well." Mr. Otto said. "But I think you can help me."

"Is she like me?"

"She's a Water Denizen, but not a Nanaue, if that's what you mean," Mr. Otto confirmed.

"Then what do you need me for?" Shawn asked. "What could I do that you can't? I mean, you're the expert."

"I think it would help her if someone closer to her own age demonstrated how the shift is supposed to happen." Mr. Otto said. "She might respond better to you than to a forty plus year old man."

"How old is she?" Shawn's voice perked up, suddenly interested. "Is she cute?"

"Don't get any ideas, she's only fourteen," Mr. Otto stated.

"Dang," Shawn said. He sighed, and then said, "how soon would you need me there?"

"If you're available, I can have you on the first plane to San Francisco tomorrow morning," Otto said.

"well, that's short notice." Shawn snarked. "Alright, sign me up. I'll get packed. How long am I going to be there for?"

"Few days, no longer."

Shawn scoffed. "Not even long enough to get over my jet lag."

"The time difference from Hawaii to California is only three hours. It's not like your flying to Australia or anything."

"Yeah, sure, whatever," Shawn said. "I guess I'll see you in the morning."

Otto presses the disconnect button and set his phone aside. He then opened his laptop, brought up a web browser, and prepared a plane ticket from Kahului to San Francisco for the early morning. The plane would leave from Hawaii at about 7:00 in the morning, and after the difference in time zones was applied, it would land at 3:00 in the afternoon. With how long it would take to get in and out of the city, he wouldn't be able to introduce Shawn and Jocelyne until the day after.

He grabbed his phone again, and this time dialed Jocelyne's number. It rang twice before she answered. "Hello?"

"Hello, Ms. Jocelyne. I called to tell you I have to cancel tomorrow's training session."

"But, why?" She asked. "I think I've gotten better. Are you giving up on me?"

"No, nothing like that." He reassured her. "You have gotten much better, but I have to make a trip to the airport tomorrow. I'm flying a friend into town, someone who can help with your transformation. But it will take all day to get him."

"Oh," she said, sounding both relieved and a little disappointed. "Who is he?"

"He's a Water Denizen like us. He's flying in from Hawaii, which is why it'll take all day to get him." Mr. Otto explained. "Don't worry too much. I'll meet you the day after tomorrow with my friend and he'll help you out."

"Okay, I guess," Jocelyne said. "What time?"

"Let's try for 12:30 at the beach. Does that work?"

"Yeah, that's fine. See you, then." She hung up the phone.

Chapter Ten

Jocelyne pushed the pedals of her bicycle backwards and came to a stop in the parking lot by the beach. Dismounting, she took the bike chain from the basket and locked it around the bike's frame and the metal rack, then glanced around the empty lot. Mr. Otto and his friend weren't here yet.

She stood on the beach, staring out over the waves crashing against the shore in a spray of white foam. Her sunglasses started to slip, she pushed them back into place. She wore cutoff jean shorts over a one piece swimsuit, blue with vertical green stripes, and flip flop sandals. Over one shoulder she carried a beach bag with her wet suit, phone, and a beach towel. She kept her hair tied back in a ponytail. Even so, a tuft of teal-green hair hung in front of her eyes. She blew it away in annoyance.

She pulled her phone out from the beach bag and checked the clock read out again. They were fifteen minutes late, Mr. Otto and whoever this person was he was bringing. She rolled her eyes, then placed the phone back in her bag and walked towards the surf. Once her towel was laid out, she sat down to wait. Mr. Otto said he was bringing someone with him today who could help with her transformation, and that she should meet them at 12:30. It was almost One and they still weren't here.

With her beach bag for a pillow, she reclined on her towel, laced her fingers together behind her head and closed her eyes to doze. Just a little nap while she waited. The crash of ocean waves filled the air and slowly lulled her into a state of pleasant contentedness.

Her dream came quickly and brought her comfort. She dreamed of the ocean, of diving beneath the waves with her arms stretched out before her and hair streaming behind her.

She breached the surface, soaring through the air for a second before plunging back into the waves. Bubbles swirled all around. A school of fish surrounded her. A dolphin came close and chirped to her before it darted away. All of this felt natural, like this was were she was supposed to be. The place she belonged.

Something nudged her shoulder. Jocelyne blinked, her dream gone, and found herself staring into the face of some unknown boy. "Morning, girly," he said with a grin, "have a nice dream?"

She sat up and scooted back, pushing his hand off her shoulder. Her heart was in her throat. She hadn't expected to wake up with someone looming over her and it freaked her out a bit.

"Jocelyne," Mr. Otto's voice called to her. She saw him standing beside his car in the small parking lot beside her bike. "Glad you made it, and sorry we're late." He wore faded white shorts with Velcro strap sandals for shoes and a floral Hawaiian shirt. Sunglasses obscured his eyes. "I'd like you to meet my friend. Jocelyne, meet Shawn."

" 'Sup," the boy, Shawn, smiled and flashed a hand sign with his thumb and pinky extended and the rest of his fingers closed. The *shaka*, if Jocelyne remembered her surfer slang correctly. She'd picked up a little of the lingo when her family briefly lived in Long Beach. "My man, Mr. Otto has told me all about you."

"Really?" Jocelyne asked, "he said nothing about you."

"Oh, yeah, it's cool." He shoved his hands back in his pockets.

Jocelyne took this moment to examine him. He was brown

skinned with short, black hair and deep brown eyes. He wore a pair of bright red swim trunks with a white leaf pattern and a white tank top under an unbuttoned orange and green Hawaiian shirt. Jocelyne, however, found her eyes drawn to the pendent that hung from his neck. It was a single tooth, large and triangular with serrated edges, it dangled from a black string, and fell flat against his chest. A shark's tooth. She let out a deep breath and a shiver ran up her back.

"He tells me you're just like me." Shawn continued, taking no notice of Jocelyne's examination. "A person of the sea."

"You're like me?" Jocelyne asked. She stood up and brushed the sand off her body. "How so?"

"Well, not exactly the same." Shawn said with a shrug. "We're both people of the ocean and can change shape in the water, but what we turn into are very different."

"So, what do you turn into?" Jocelyne placed her hands on her hips and arched an eyebrow.

"Doesn't matter right now." Mr. Otto interrupted. "He's here to help you with your transformation."

"I don't need any help. I've been doing just fine on my own." Jocelyne crossed her arms. She was being defensive, and knew it. With all the time she'd been practicing, she still hadn't made any real progress towards her first transformation. Sure, she could swim faster than anyone else, see clearly underwater, and hold her breath for up to half an hour, but she couldn't transform.

"Doing just fine, huh?" Shawn said. "Maybe you can show me. Let's swim out together and change."

Jocelyne turned her back to him and adjusted her sunglasses, trying in vain to hide her embarrassed blush. "Don't want to."

"Don't want to, or can't?" Shawn asked, and Jocelyne could hear the smirk. The back of her neck warmed with anger and embarrassment. Her shoulders hunched and tightened.

"Don't tease, Shawn," Mr. Otto called to them. "She's having a difficult enough time without being made fun off. Now, come along," he opened the car door and slid into the driver's seat, "we need to get to the pier before our boat reservation expires."

"Boat reservation?" Jocelyne picked up her towel, shook it a few times to get the sand off, then rolled it up and stuffed it into her bag. Shawn walked by her side back to the car.

"Yeah," the surfer-looking boy said as he slipped into the front seat. "We're going out to sea today. We're going to try your transformation in deeper water."

Jocelyne tossed her bag into the car and then climbed into the back. "Do you think that's been the problem?" She asked, directing her question towards Mr. Otto. "The water hasn't been deep enough?"

"At this point, I'm willing to try anything." The pepper-haired man turned the key and the car's engine rumbled to life. "Did you bring your Changeling Suit?" Otto asked.

"Of course," Jocelyne patted her beach bag.

"Good. You'll both need to change clothes when we get to the harbor. There won't be a place on the boat." Otto pulled out of the parking lot and they drove in silence towards the boat harbor.

Chapter Eleven

The boat engine's rumble softened until it came to a low, idling, metal hum. Mr. Otto swiveled around in his chair to address the two teenagers seated on the benches that ran the back half of the boat. "This is far enough," he said. "Time to get out, kids."

"Here?" Jocelyne looked over the back of the boat, the stern, and couldn't see the mainland anywhere. "How far out are we?"

"About five miles." Mr. Otto explained. "That may seem far, but we're just barely out of visual range of the shore. I figured you'd like a little privacy for your first transformation."

"You really think it'll work this time?" Jocelyne asked.

"If this doesn't do it, nothing will." Mr. Otto turned to Shawn.

"Now, be patient with her, she's been having some trouble with the first shift."

"I remember." Shawn slipped his shark tooth necklace off and set it on the towel beside him. He stood and stretched his arms high over his head, then twisted his torso first to the left and then to the right. He wore a wetsuit similar to Jocelyne's, with the same charcoal and ash gray, but with streaks of deep red that started at the ankles and wound all the way up to the shoulders. He gave Jocelyne another cocky smile. "You ready for this?"

"Absolutely!" She was on her feet in an instant. Taking a hair tie, she fixed her hair back in a pony-tail again. She wore her teal and gray Changeling Suit. "Let's do this."

Shawn nodded with a smirk. "Alright." He braced his foot on the ledge of the boat and leaped into the water. He disappeared beneath the surface.

Jocelyne followed. She sprinted three long strides across the boat's deck then dove and allowed the ocean to engulf her. Bubbles streamed all around as she kicked up and down, picking up speed. She opened her eyes and looked around, but couldn't see Shawn. Her vision was clear, as if she wore goggles, but he was nowhere to be seen.

She breached the surface, swinging her head around to whip the hair away from her face, and inhaled deeply. Her arms and legs swished back and forth to keep her afloat.

"How's the water?" Mr. Otto called to her from the boat. Jocelyne turned around to see him a fair distance away, maybe fifty yards. She'd swam that far away already? Maybe her swimming speed was getting better.

"Water's fine!" She shouted back. In actuality, it was a little cold for her liking, but her wetsuit made it alright. "I don't see where Shawn went, though!"

"Don't worry, he's around!" Mr. Otto said. "I'm going to move the boat a little further away, and you need to swim back to it. Think you can do that?"

"Of course!" Jocelyne raised one hand from the water and gave a thumbs up.

"Good." Mr. Otto seated himself at the steering wheel again and pushed the throttle lever. The boat rumbled as it picked up speed and sailed away.

Jocelyne took a deep breath and dove beneath the waves again. On the surface, the water was choppy, but underneath it was almost calm. She kicked and pushed her way through the water, like it was second nature to her, as easy as breathing. In the ocean, she was more at home than she'd ever been on land, even with her brothers.

She swam towards the boat. She could see the twisting water made by its propeller and hear the drone of its engine. Even though it moved faster than her, she knew at some point Mr. Otto would slow and stop. Seemed to be taking him a while, though.

In mid-stroke, she saw a shadow pass by just out of her sight. She paused and turned to look just as whatever it was disappeared in deeper, darker waters with a swish of its tail.

A bolt of fear shot through Jocelyne like lightning. She thought of that day at the aquarium, when she jumped into the tank to rescue her brother. She kicked harder, pushing herself faster towards the boat. Looking ahead, she saw that Mr. Otto still hadn't shut the engine off. He was moving further away with each passing moment.

Jocelyne surfaced for a quick breath, and looking behind her, saw a familiar and horrifying sight. A triangular fin, slate colored and slick with water, cut like a knife through the ocean's surface. Taking a breath again, she dunked her head underwater for a better look. She had to be sure, needed to know for certain this was what she feared.

It was. Less than a hundred feet away, advancing towards her with an almost graceful side to side motion, was the torpedo shaped body, and powerful jaws of a Great White shark.

Her mind was lost in a haze of pure panic. She couldn't move, or even breathe, only stare at the large fish as it came closer with each back and forth motion of its crescent tail. Jocelyne couldn't think, only feel the word shark.

This shark was much larger than the one from the aquarium, at least twice the size. Jocelyne was there again, back in that tank, following the trail of blood flowing from Travis's eviscerated leg, just as the rows of teeth rushed towards her. She could still hear the bone-chilling crunch as those jaws closed inches from her face.

These memories came back so strong and with such intensity, that Jocelyne was moving before she knew. She spun around in the water, turning away from the shark. Her legs came together like a mock tail and kicked, driving her in the direction of the boat.

It seemed further away now. She could still hear the drone of the boat's motor, but it was more distant than before. And Mr. Otto wasn't slowing. "Hey!" She threw one arm out of the water and tried to wave him down. "Stop! Come back!" Her throat was raw from screaming and the salt water.

Mr. Otto must've seen her, since Jocelyne saw him wave back. But he did not stop the boat. Nor did he turn back to help her or even slow. Did he not see the shape in the water behind her? The knife-like fin of the shark as it sliced through the surface?

No help was coming. She was alone out here, stranded at sea with a blood-thirsty predator coming for her. That reality began to set in and Jocelyne felt a new level of fear envelope her. Not the initial burst of panic like before, but something much deeper and more primal. An existential terror she hadn't felt since that day in the aquarium tank. She was alone, and that frightened her more than any shark could.

Jocelyne would have to save herself. Getting to that boat was the only chance she had. Her fists clenched and jaw tightened with this new resolve. She pulled her legs close, then thrust them back, propelling herself forward like a shot. Arm over arm, kicking up and down, she swam forward with more vigor and speed than she knew she had.

She held her arms close to her body, using just her legs to push herself through the water. Bubbles swirled all around her. She felt a change take over, something like the first time she swam to escape a shark, but stronger and more pronounced than before. She let it happened, embraced it, consumed it, wrapped herself in it like a blanket. No, closer than a blanket. Like it was her own skin and she had never known.

The boat was very close now, directly in front of her. Only now, as she was just behind the stern, did the propeller slow. Jocelyne burst from the water and tried to reach for the boat, but her arms were too short. She clapped her hands in the water, stretching but not reaching the lips of the boat. She tried to shout, but the only sound to come from her mouth was a yelping bark.

Mr. Otto's face appeared over the edge of the boat and he smiled down at her. "Aha! It looks like it worked!" He said. His hand slapped the side of the boat. "Come on, then, you can jump this easy."

Jocelyne let herself slip back underwater. Looking around, she saw the shark still coming towards her, but not as fast as before. Even so, she wanted away from it. She twisted in the water, and found it was easier than she remembered. She dove a little ways deeper, then turned around and leapt out of the surface.

Her body landed with a wet thud on the bottom of the boat. She tried to stand, and found she couldn't. She could only lie there on her stomach.

"You did it!" Mr. Otto laughed, his hands slapped on his knees. "Congratulations, you achieved your first selkie shift."

The boat jolted roughly at the stern. Jocelyne looked and a new wave of terror washed over her. The shark had leapt out of the water and somehow hooked its fins over the back of the boat. It thrashed and struggled, pulling itself up.

She wanted to run, still couldn't, and instead found herself flopping across the deck away from the snapping jaws of the shark. The huge fish managed to get enough of itself over the edge that it teetered forward and fell inside. It lay with its face pressed against the bottom of the boat and its tail waving comically in the air. Only then, did it start to change.

The tail split down the middle, almost like the shark was being torn in half, and Jocelyne saw them become legs. The dorsal fin shrank and the two front fins grew first into hands, and then whole arms. The gills melded together into flat skin.

The head changed the most. The pointed snout shrank until it was just a human nose, the teeth became small and flat, eyes shifted from the sides to the front of the face, and a mop of black hair sprouted atop its head.

Shawn! The shark had become Shawn!

He propped himself up on his knees and snatched his towel off the bench. He still wore the red and black, skin-tight wetsuit from before. "You know," he said, "I don't think you needed my help all that much." He took his shark tooth necklace from the bench, beside where his towel used to lay, and looped it around his neck again. "You figured out the skin changing thing pretty easily, seal girl."

Jocelyne still couldn't believe her eyes. The shark had been Shawn all along. And Mr. Otto knew it!

Chapter Twelve

Mr. Otto helmed the boat. Waves crashed against the hull as they sailed towards shore. Jocelyne sat on the port side bench, her towel draped across her shoulders. Her wet hair clung to her face and neck.

Shawn sat across from her on the starboard bench with his foot resting across his knee. He still had that same grin, which Jocelyne had come to hate. She hadn't spoken to either Shawn or Mr. Otto since reverting back. They tried offering congratulations on her first shifting, but once her seal skin had shed she clammed up. She sat in silence with her arms wrapped around her knees and eyes fixed on the floor of the boat. Her selkie skin rested on the bench beside her, neatly folded like a pair of pajamas. Jocelyne brushed her fingers against it, feeling the softness of the fur. It was as much a part of her as her arm was. Occasionally she would look up and meet Shawn's gaze, but each time she shot him a death glare and turned away.

For a long time, no one said anything, The only sounds came from the boat motor and the waves crashing against the bow. At long last, Shawn spoke. "Okay, what's with the attitude? You got something you want to say, say it already. Are you mad you didn't get the form you wanted? Did you think you were a mermaid or something? Let me tell you something, mermaids are overrated. Smug, self-absorbed brats, that's all mermaids are. There's nothing wrong with a selkie."

Jocelyne pushed out her lower lip and turned away, pulling her towel tighter around her shoulders.

"Fine. Be like that." Shawn crossed his arms and faced the other direction. "You're welcome, by the way."

"You don't understand," Jocelyne muttered under her breath. "You're all the same. All of you."

"What was that?" Shawn leaned forward. "You finally got the nerve to say something? Well, speak up, already. Can't hear you with that mumble."

"You're just like the rest!" Jocelyne found herself suddenly shouting. She jumped to her feet, her hands clenched into fists. The towel fell away. "All of you! All you know how to do is torment and criticize! You know nothing about me, who do you think you are to pass judgment!?"

Shawn sat dumbstruck, his eyes wide in shock. He blinked in confusion.

Jocelyne slumped back to the bench. She let out a sigh, then spoke in a quieter voice. "When I was little, my brother and I were attacked by a Great White shark," she explained. "They had one at the Pacific Bay Aquarium years ago and my little brother fell into the tank. It grabbed him by the leg and dragged him underwater. I dove in without thinking to rescue him, and it tried to eat me. Somehow I made it out okay, but my brother lost half his leg."

Tears peaked at the corners of her eyes. Her lips quivered and shoulders began to shake. "It was my idea to go to the aquarium. I lost track of my brothers. It's my fault he got hurt." She started to cry and buried her face in her arms. "I still have nightmares sometimes. I see blood in the water, hear my four-year-old brother scream for help as he's dragged below. And the teeth, all those horrible teeth." She shuddered. "I can't handle it. And no one cares to help me. It's all too much."

Shawn found himself speechless. He stared back at this girl baring her soul and crying her eyes out, and for the first time, didn't know what to say. A pit formed in his stomach the longer he stayed quiet. Had they just traumatized this girl to force her selkie skin to appear? He now realized why she freaked out over the tattoo on his back. It took a long time before he could bring himself to speak again. "I'm sorry," he said at last, "I didn't know about you or your brother. I wouldn't have done it if I knew."

"I don't care," Jocelyne said, still looking away. "It's still wrong."

"Wait a minute," Shawn's eyebrows rose as he was hit with a thought. He turned towards the bow to address Mr. Otto. "Did you know about what happened to her?"

"Of course I did," the older man answered without hesitation. "That's why I brought you here."

"What!?" Shawn was on his feet in an instant. He stormed up to the front of the boat, grabbed the throttle lever and forced it down. The boat motor slowed before it choked and died. "You knew about her past experience with sharks and called me in anyway?"

"That's exactly the reason why I did," Mr. Otto stood and

turned to address the teenagers. "We were at an impasse, a sink or swim moment. Time was running out and if you didn't grow your skin soon, you never would've," he said to Jocelyne. "The only time you experienced any of your selkie abilities was when your life was in danger."

"So you thought it would work to put me in that kind of situation again?" She lashed back, the tears still wet on her cheeks.

"Shawn would never hurt you," he turned from the girl to the young Hawaiian, "would you?"

"Of course not." Shawn denied.

Mr. Otto turned back to Jocelyne, "Then you were never in any real danger. Of course, I couldn't let you know that. I figured you needed to experience the same raw fear as you had that day to push through your mental block and shift for the first time." He smiled and gave his thigh a slap. "And it worked! You have your skin, you're a full blown selkie now!"

"But she's right. It was still wrong," Shawn said forcefully. "You used me. And you took advantage of her condition,"

"If I hadn't, she never would've gotten her skin," Mr. Otto said. He turned to Jocelyne, his voice was gentler than before. "Child, you deserve to know the truth and experience your heritage the same as anyone else. Your mother is still out there waiting to meet you, and I promised her I'd reunite you two. But you needed to achieve your selkie skin first."

"Why?" Jocelyne wiped her tears away, anger still resonated in her voice.

"I'm sorry, but I still can't say. Not yet." Mr. Otto said.

"All these secrets!" Jocelyne lashed out. "Everyone is keeping secrets from me! Why can't anyone just tell me the truth?"

"I will," Mr. Otto said. "In time, if you allow me, I'll tell you everything. But we have a few more steps to go before we get there."

Jocelyne pushed herself off the bench again, her hands grasped around the seal skin. "If that's the case, I don't want this stupid thing!" She turned to the stern of the boat and lifted the skin over her head, making as if to throw it.

"No! Don't!" Shawn shouted.

She couldn't. A part of her wanted to, but her fingers would not let go. Jocelyne pulled the skin close and clutched it tight. It was warm and soft, like holding the pet she never had.

Shawn and Otto both sighed in relief. Shawn placed a hand over his chest and could feel his racing heart. He stepped over to her, placing one hand on her shoulder and running his other across the seal fur. "You have to keep this safe. If anyone should take it, they could use it to control you. It's happened to selkies across the ages."

"He speaks true." Mr. Otto confirmed. He took his seat at the steering wheel again and started the motor. The propeller spun as the inboard motor rumbled to life. Jocelyne and Shawn took their seats and they continued heading back towards shore.

At the port, Mr. Otto pulled the small boat back into the marina and went to talk with the shipyard owner. Jocelyne and Shawn were left on the dock waiting for him. "I really am sorry," Shawn said.

"Apology accepted," Jocelyne replied. She had her selkie skin wrapped up in her towel and tucked under her arm. The strap of her beach bag hung from her shoulder, carrying her other clothes and personals. "So, do shark shifters have a special name like selkies do?"

"Sort of," Shawn admitted. "The first shark man of Hawaii was Nanaue, the son of Kamohoalii, king of all sharks and one of many ocean gods. It's said on the night Nanaue was born there was a terrible storm that ravaged the island. And his mother noticed he had a gaping shark mouth on his back. All shark men can trace their line back to him. So I suppose you could call us Nanaue. Or weresharks if that's easier."

Jocelyne laughed. Her first real laugh since getting on that boat. "Is that what the necklace is for?" She asked. "A sign of your heritage?"

"Not in the way you're thinking." Shawn hooked a thumb under the string and lifted the shark tooth. "This is one of mine. I keep my old teeth and make necklaces out of them to sell to tourists."

"That's really clever." Jocelyne admitted.

"Alright, kids," Mr. Otto called as he came out of the marina office, "time to go. I've got to get you home."

The pair of teens climbed into the back of Mr. Otto's car and he drove them back to the beach where Jocelyne had locked her bike. As she was getting out, Shawn called her name.

"Jocelyne," he stretched out his hand. "Here, let me give you my number. If you need anything, call me. Consider it my way of apologizing for scaring you."

Jocelyne managed to dig her phone out of her travel bag and handed it over to Shawn. He gave her his phone in exchange.

The background on Shawn's home screen was a picture of him in swim shorts carrying a surfboard and flashing the *hang loose* sign. He was shirtless in the picture, the shark tooth hanging from his neck. Jocelyne opened his contacts. After putting in her number, she closed the display and handed the phone back in a hurry.

Shawn took back his phone and returned Jocelyne's. He walked back to the other side of the car and climbed inside."Give me a call if you need anything," he said. After closing the doors, Mr. Otto pulled away from the curb and drove back towards town.

Jocelyne stood alone on the beach, her phone weighed heavily in her hand. She listened to the crashing of waves against the shore and the cawing of sea birds. She stuck her phone back in her bag and headed back to where her bike was chained up. Setting the bag in the front basket, she unlocked the bike, hopped into the seat and started pedaling back home.

Chapter Thirteen

As she approached the house, Jocelyne spotted Shannon standing on the front porch. The woman leaned against one of the support beams of the overhang, with her arms crossed and a disapproving scowl on her face. The closer she came, the more Jocelyne's heart started to sink. She slowed her pedaling and brought the bike to a stop at the foot of the stairs leading up to the porch. "Is something wrong?" She asked as she dismounted and pulled her beach bag out of the basket.

"Come inside." Shannon gestured to the door. "Your father and I need to discuss some things with you."

"Can I at least lock the bike up?" Jocelyne asked, desperate to delay any interaction with the adults of the house.

"After we've talked with you." Shannon said. "Inside, now."

She leaned her bike against the porch, slung the strap of her beach bag over her shoulders, then trudged up the steps to the front door and into the living room, where Ben was waiting.

He stood in the middle of the room, his arms crossed over his chest and eyes filled with more scorn than his wife. Jocelyne could already feel the heat rising up her neck, the disapproving anger all over the parental figure's faces. "Sit." Ben commanded and motioned to the couch where Jacob and Travis were already seated.

Jocelyne sat beside her brothers, the beach bag rested on her lap and her eyes focused on the carpet, as if that would avoid the adults anger. She didn't even know what they were angry about. "What's going on?" She whispered to Travis.

"We're sorry," he hushed back, "they asked about you, and we kinda confessed."

The front door closed and Shannon moved to stand beside her husband. Both adults glared down at the three children. For a long while, nobody talked. The wall clock steadily ticked away the painful seconds. At long last, Ben finally said, "So, which one of you wants to tell me why you're all here?"

None of the kids said anything. They didn't even look at one another, only sat on the couch and stared at the floor.

"Really? None of you have anything to say?" Ben scolded. "Especially you, Jocelyne."

She winced at the mention of her name. Her shoulders hunched and grip tightened around the bag in her lap. She shifted her eyes up and was met with Ben's judgmental gaze. A part of her felt ashamed, but as they stared at one another, something deeper wanted confrontation. "Anything to say about what?"

"Don't take that tone with me, young lady." Ben snapped, making Jocelyne tense up again. "I know what you've been getting up to. And what you've been doing."

"If you know, then why did you want me to fess up?" Jocelyne asked, growing bolder. She wanted a fight, wanted to shout, and scream.

"I was giving you a chance." Ben said. "But it's clear you don't care. I called your friends and none of them have seen you in the last week."

"Maybe I made new friends you don't know about." She sassed.

"Not only that," Ben continued without acknowledging her words, "I also know you've been sneaking out."

"You ungrounded me!" Jocelyne snapped.

"You were doing it before that." Ben stated. "Did you think we wouldn't notice you disappearing for hours at a time?"

Her lips twisted into a grimace and her brows furled. "Why do you care anyways?"

"Because I'm your father." Ben unfolded his arms and placed one hand on his hips, then pointed at Jocelyne and said in a stern voice, "And I don't appreciate your keeping secrets from me."

"Secrets?" The word set off something in Jocelyne. A string wound too tight that finally snapped. "Maybe we should talk about some secrets. Like the ones you've been keeping from me my whole life!" She suddenly found herself shouting, and didn't care.

"Don't raise you voice at me, Jocelyne!" Ben snapped back. "I am your father, and I – "

"No, you're not!" Jocelyne screamed again. She jumped off the couch, her hair flew around her face and anger burned in her eyes. "You're not my father!" She turned to Shannon. "And you aren't my mother! I know the truth!"

The whole house fell silent. Ben and Shannon's eyes grew wide with shock. They glanced at each other, and then back to Jocelyne. The twins stared in stark disbelief. "What did you just say?" Shannon said at last.

"I know who I am, and what I am!" She slung her beach bag across her back. "And you can't keep me here anymore!" Jocelyne raced past the adults and flung the front door open. Before she could run, a hand clutched around her bag

"Jocelyne, wait a minute!" Shannon exclaimed, holding her back. "We can talk about this!"

"Don't touch me!" She reached back and grabbed at the zipper, she caught it and nearly tore the bag open. Her towel, change of clothes, cell phone, and selkie skin fell out in a pile on the floor. Jocelyne took the bag off and snatched her seal skin. She bounded down the porch steps in a single leap, jumped on her bike, and rode off into the night. She clicked on the bike's headlight and a beam of white light flooded across the street in front of her.

Shannon stood in the doorway. She stared at the items left in a heap on the floor, her lips parted in shock. "I saw it." She turned back to her husband with the empty beach bag clutched in her hand.

"Saw what?" Ben asked.

"Her skin." Shannon's voice trembled as she spoke. "I saw it fall out when she opened the bag. A selkie skin."

"That's impossible." Ben proclaimed. "We haven't told her."

"But I saw it." Shannon threw the bag to the floor, marched back to where her purse sat beside the kitchen door, and grabbed her keys. "We have to go after her."

Ben nodded. "Come on, boys." He ordered as he grabbed his coat. "We're going to track down your sister."

"Okay, hold on a minute!" Jacob leaped off the couch. "Would someone mind explaining what just happened? What was she screaming about?"

"We don't have time right now." Ben said. "We'll explain everything when we get her back. Now, come on."

They streamed out of the house and into the car; the kids in back, mom on the passenger side, and dad driving. The car rumbled to life and the headlights flashed. They pulled out of the driveway fast enough for the tires to screech and sped after Jocelyne. It wasn't long before they caught up to her, following the single bike light.

Jocelyne pedaled furiously, her legs pumping up and down as she accelerated. She didn't know exactly where she was going, but she knew where this road led. Her selkie skin sat in the basket on the front of the bike. The sea was what called to her, so the sea was where she'd go.

A pair of bright lights shined behind her. She glanced over

her shoulder to see the car, then swerved to one side of the road to let it pass. Instead, the car pulled alongside and slowed. "Jocelyne!" Ben Chambers shouted from inside the car. It was too dark to see him, but she knew his voice. "Stop this, right now!"

Up ahead, the road gave way to the fine sand dunes and crashing waves of the beach. Jocelyne veered off to this side, grabbed her selkie skin out of the basket, and threw the bike to the sand. Behind her, the car pulled off the road. Its headlights shone on her as she ran for the water's edge. "Jocelyne!" They shouted her name again when they stepped out of the car. She didn't care. She kicked off her shoes and raced into the water.

"Jocy!" A new voice, younger and more innocent, shouted for her. She stopped in the crashing wake of ankle deep water, her selkie skin draped across her back. "Please, don't go away!" She turned around to see the shadows of her brothers, Travis and Jacob, standing beside the car.

"We're sorry, Jocy," the first one, Travis, called to her, "We didn't mean to tell on you."

"Don't be angry with us!" The second, Jacob, continued.

"I'm not mad at you," Jocelyne shouted back, pulling at the flippers of her seal skin as though they were the sleeves of a

152

jacket.

"Then why are you running away?" Jacob cried.

"I can't stay here." Jocelyne took a step back, the water swirled around her legs. "I'm sorry." She tore away from them, pushing her way into the crashing surf.

"Wait!" The boys screamed and ran down the beach after her. Jacob pulled ahead with Travis hobbling behind on his broken prosthetic.

"Don't leave – Oof!" Travis's fake leg twisted in the uneven sand and he fell, landing sprawled out on the beach. Jacob stopped running and turned back to his twin. Jocelyne glanced back one last time, seeing her little brother lying on his stomach with an arm reached out for her, then shut her eyes with a fierce desire to stave off any incoming tears, and dove beneath the surface.

Waves crashed against the sandy beach, a spray of sea foam and salt lingered in the air. Ben and Shannon Chambers stood by the open doors of their car, staring into the light cast by the car's high beams, waiting for Jocelyne to surface. She never did.

Ben slammed his fist down on the top of the car. "Damn it!" He cursed, but his tone betrayed an inner grief. "Why did she run away now? How did she find out about us? How did she even get her selkie skin?"

Shannon slipped listlessly back into the car, her mouth hung open in shock. Her hands settled into her lap and she found herself staring at them. As the gravity of what had just happened began to settle, her lips quivered and eyes watered until she could no longer restrain herself, and she sobbed into her hands.

Jacob helped Travis to his feet. He pulled his twin's arm across his shoulders, and carried the prosthetic leg with his free hand. The brothers came to sit in the backseat of the car. They looked from one parent to another, from their fuming father to the weeping mother.

"What just happened?" Jacob asked.

Ben sighed and ran a hand through his hair. He pulled the lever beside the driver's seat that opened the trunk, and then walked to where Jocelyne had tossed her bike. It wouldn't fit perfectly, but just enough to get it home.

"Dad," Jacob called, "Jocelyne just jumped into the ocean and hasn't come back. You and Mom know something. What is it?"

"Just put your seat belts on," Ben said. His tone was full of defeat. He started the car, reversed it off the beach, then drove back to the house.

Chapter Fourteen

The water was black as ink. Jocelyne couldn't see the sea floor beneath her, and the only sounds came from the crashing surf. She was going south, as far as she knew, keeping the coastline to her left, and never venturing far from shore. Her back flippers swayed from side to side, pushing her along at a steady pace.

Where was she hoping to go? She had no money, no phone, no shoes or clothes aside from the Changeling suit. Did she even have a plan after running away? The answer, of course, was no. And because of that, she was now in her seal form, swimming down the ocean coast in the middle of the night.

She surfaced for breath, a burst of misty air puffed from her nostrils, and scanned the coastline. The highway ran along the beach, and cars occasionally sped by, their headlights casting shadows on the guardrails across the sand. The bright, fluorescent lights of a trunk stop gas station and a fast food joint burned a little further south from where she swam. She could see the rows of semis lined up beside the building along with the signs of the service station and golden arches of a McDonald's restaurant.

Jocelyne swam to the beach and as she crawled on land, her skin sloughed away. She returned to a human shape. Picking up the seal skin, she rolled it in a bundle and tucked it under her arm before walking towards the gas station. She needed a phone, and to call the only person she could trust right now: Otto.

The truck stop was further away than she expected. She had to climb over the guardrail and walk along the side of the highway for nearly half a mile before crossing the street. Her feet ached from the rough asphalt and tiny pebbles of the road. When she finally got there, pushing open the door of the burger place, and getting a blast of cold air to the face, she was exhausted.

The young lady working the register looked over at her. "Um, hello? Can I help you?"

Jocelyne brushed a strand of wet, teal hair away from her face. "Yeah," she walked to the counter, her feet made wet, popping noises with each step. "Can I use your phone?"

"Uh," the young lady stuttered, "yeah, hold on, let me ask my manager." She stepped away from the register and walked deeper into the store. Jocelyne could hear her and the boss talking. As she waited, she looked back at the other customers. Some were staring at her, others pretended to not care.

The cashier and manager came back, a cordless phone nestled in the manager woman's hand. "Good evening," the older, larger, woman said. She looked tired, her blonde hair with long, gray roots tied back in a bun, and a headset over ear. "Who do you need to call?"

"My," Jocelyne fumbled for a moment. What was she supposed to say? Friend? Teacher? Octopus man? "Uncle," she said at last.

"We're quite a ways out of town. How'd you get all the way out here?" The manager continued her probe of questions.

Jocelyne noticed the suspicious looks of the employees, and knew she had to come up with a story. Something to explain why she was walking along the side of the highway at night with nothing but a wetsuit and a bundled up seal skin. "I was out swimming," she lied, "and while I was in the water, some freak came down from his car and took my bag. Just grabbed it and drove off, can you believe it?"

The lie was coming to her so swiftly now, she almost felt guilty. "And that bag had everything. My clothes, my cash, sandals, phone, and the keys to my bike lock. I shouted at him, but by the time I climbed back onto shore he'd already gotten back in his car and peeled out down the road. I swear, the people in this town."

"Alright," the manager handed Jocelyne the cordless phone.

"Thank you." She took the phone and after thinking for a minute, dialed Mr. Otto's number. It was a good thing she'd committed his number to memory.

Three buzzes and a click later, Otto's voice came from the speaker. "Hello?"

"Hi, Uncle Otto," Jocelyne said, catching herself as she spoke.

"Jocelyne?" He asked, a level of confusion in his voice, probably from being called 'uncle'. "I wasn't expecting to hear from you again today. My contacts didn't display your number, so it confused me."

"Yeah, I'm not calling from my phone." Jocelyne admitted.

"Can you come pick me up?"

"Why?" Otto asked, confused. "What happened?"

"Kinda a long story." She said. "I'll explain when you get here. Can you just come get me?"

"How am I supposed to? I don't know where you are."

"I don't know exactly where, either," Jocelyne admitted, "I'm at a McDonald's in a truck stop off the highway. Someplace north of San Francisco."

"Alright." Otto said. "I'll search for this in my maps and come get you. Just sit tight for a while."

"Kay, thanks. See you soon." She pressed the disconnect button and handed the phone back to the clerk. "Thank you. Can I get a water cup?"

The girl exchanged a small cup for the phone. Jocelyne took the cup, filled it with water, and waited in a booth by the window.

It was nearly forty-five minutes before the familiar shape of the red Ford Focus pulled into the parking lot. Jocelyne was on her feet and moving for the door just as Mr. Otto walked inside. "Good evening, Ms. Chambers."

"Hi, Uncle," she reiterated, trying to push the notion. "Glad you could come get me."

"What was I supposed to do? I wasn't going to leave you stranded out here," he said. "You hungry?"

"Yes, actually," Jocelyne said, realizing she was not only hungry, but downright starving.

"Okay, you sit tight, I'm going to get you something." He walked to the counter and placed an order for a bunch of cheeseburgers, a couple of drinks, and some fries. While Jocelyne waited with the receipt, Otto ventured into the convenience store section and then came back with a pair of flip-flops. By the time he returned, their food was ready.

"So, tell me what happened?" Otto handed her the flip-flops, then sat across from her and placed his hands together on the table. "What are you doing all the way out here?"

Jocelyne had to pause while she swallowed her mouthful of cheeseburger. She took a quick sip of soda, then explained what happened. How she fought with the adults, ran out of the house, biked down to the beach, and escaped into the ocean. She finished her story with how she got to the McDonald's.

"I see," Otto said, and Jocelyne could see the wheels turning in his head. "That's going to change things."

"Change what?" She asked.

"Our timeline." Mr. Otto walked back to the counter and got

a to-go bag. He began filling it with the uneaten burgers and fries. "I was planning on waiting a little while for you to practice with your new abilities, but we don't have that luxury anymore." He glanced at the ceiling and spoke as an aside. "It would've also helped with ticket prices."

"Tickets?"

"Come on," He said as he dumped the trash in a bin and set the tray on top. "I'll tell you on the way." They rushed out to the car, Jocelyne sat in the passenger seat with her selkie skin laying across her lap. Mr. Otto set his phone into the dashboard phone mount and dialed the airport. He set it to speaker mode.

"Good evening. San Francisco International Airport. How can I help you?" A woman's voice answered from the speaker.

"I need the first flight you have to the U.K." Otto said as he pulled out of the parking lot. "Do you have any flights going to Glasgow or Edinburgh?"

"How soon do you want to fly?" The voice asked.

"Tonight."

"I will check, but this is really late notice." The voice replied, and Jocelyne thought she could hear annoyance in the woman's tone. There was a clattering of computer keys, and then the voice said, "We have a plane going out to Edinburgh tonight at 11:30.

It only has one seat left, and it is rather expensive."

"That's fine, I'll take it." Otto said.

"Alright, I'll register you. And what is the name?"

"Jocelyne McNeal." Otto said.

Jocelyne's eyes shot wide open and her lips parted upon hearing her name. Flying? To Edinburgh? Alone? What was going on?

"Is the traveling person a minor?"

"She is. There will be someone in Edinburgh to pick her up." Otto said. "I'll pay in cash at the airport." He and the airport receptionist exchanged a few more questions before everything was settled and he pressed the disconnect button. "You're flying back home tonight." he said, the first direct sentence he'd spoken to Jocelyne since they got in the car.

"I gathered that." She said. "But why not tomorrow morning?"

"Has to be tonight." Otto confirmed. "If we wait too long, your foster parents will report you as a runaway and the authorities will be searching. If you still want to know your real parents, you'll have to do it tonight."

"But I don't have anything with me." Jocelyne protested. "I have no clothes, no money, I don't even have a passport. How am I supposed to fly to another country?"

"Reach into the back." Otto directed. "I have my briefcase back there."

Jocelyne craned her head back and saw it resting on the back seat. She snatched it and brought it up to lay on her lap. "Got it," she said.

"The combination is already set. Open it."

Jocelyne pressed the two buttons and the latches snapped up. She lifted it open and found a maroon-red booklet with golden imprints. The imprint was of a coat of arms flanked on one side by a lion and on the other by a unicorn. The words above it read *Kingdom of Great Britain and Northern Ireland*. Flipping the booklet open, she found her picture staring back at her, along with the name *Jocelyne McNeal*. "How did you get this?"

"Your parents had it made before they even hired me." Otto explained. "In preparation to bring you home."

Jocelyne looked down at the passport in her hands. She opened it again to look at her picture, and at her name. She flipped through the pages, all blank and awaiting stamps.

Jocelyne didn't know what to feel. The drive to the airport was both too long, and too short. Getting there, even getting a new change of clothes so she could stop wearing the Changeling suit, seemed to pass in a blur. Before she knew it, she was sitting at the gate, waiting for the plane to refuel and the passengers to unload before she could board. She stared out the large window as luggage was loaded onto the plane. She held her boarding pass and passport in both hands, her new backpack containing her selkie skin and Changeling suit sat on the seat beside her.

Her boarding group was called. Jocelyne stood and waited in line, handed the boarding pass to the receptionist, who scanned it and then gave it back to her. Once finally on the plane, she sat by a window and looked out over the wing. Only when the plane began to move and the force of take-off pressed her back against the seat, did she accept what was happening. Everything she'd ever known was behind her. The world, the truth, lay ahead.

Chapter Fifteen

Shannon was on the couch, her hands folded in her lap. She seemed to stare at the floor, but wasn't looking at it at all. Her mind was miles away, emotions lost in a dense fog of numbness. Ben had gone off to the kitchen, grabbed a beer from the fridge, and chugged it. He now sat at the dinner table, two empty bottles before him, a third in his hand, and stared blankly at the wall.

The twins, after trying to wrestle some kind of explanation from their parents and failing, retreated to their room. Travis sat on the bottom bunk of the bunk beds and Jacob rested in the gaming chair by their desk. Travis clutched Jocelyne's discarded phone in his hands.

"Do you think it's something we did?" Travis asked. "Did we

say or do something to make her leave?"

"I don't know." Jacob leaned back in his chair. "Doesn't matter, anyway. She's gone. She jumped in the ocean and drowned."

"I don't think so." Travis pressed the oval button on the bottom of the phone and the screen lit up. "She was shouting about things before leaving. Saying, like Mom and Dad aren't her real Mom and Dad or some crazy things like that." He looked up at his twin. "What do you think she meant by that?"

"Again, I don't know." Jacob swiveled his chair around, trying to ignore his brother.

"You remember the key?" Travis continued. "The one we gave her so she would take us to that movie?"

"She never took us." Jacob muttered.

"She wanted it to see something in the attic. Do you think she found it?"

"I really don't care." Jacob opened a drawer in his computer desk and pulled out a large set of headphones. He slipped them over his ears and turned on the computer to drown out his twin's questioning. Jacob was troubled, but he didn't want to think about it. If he did, it would only upset him more. Maybe it would all work out if he just ignored it.

Travis set Jocelyne's phone on the bed beside him, then stood up. His fake leg squeaked and groaned as he walked down the hall to her room. If no one would help him, he would find the answers himself.

He knew Jocelyne didn't drown when she ran into the ocean. He couldn't explain why, he just knew it. He and his sister had a special bond, one not shared with Jacob. Travis was obviously close to Jacob because they were twins, but with Jocelyne it was something else. Something that happened in that aquarium when they were little kids.

Turning on her bedroom light, he found her room to be a mess, clothes lying everywhere and a bed with the blankets kicked off. A book sat on the bedside table with a bookmark sticking out at the halfway point. He walked over to the bed and sat on it. Maybe, if he could see things from her point of view, he could learn why she ran away.

His foot nudged something under the bed. Looking down, Travis spotted the corner of a white photo album. Intrigued, he pulled it out, set it in his lap, and flipped it open.

At first, the pictures looked boring, just a man and woman taking snapshots of dates, vacation pics, and wedding photos. That is until he found pictures of his parents mixed in with the other couple. There were even a few pictures of all four of them together. The last photo, however, both shocked and confused him. The woman was in a hospital bed with a newborn in her arms. Surrounding her was the woman's husband and Travis's own parents, the caption below read Happy Birthday, Jocelyne.

Travis slammed the book shut, jumped off the bed, and marched down the hall towards the living room. He paused along the way to get Jacob. "Come on," he said, all but pulling his twin from the computer chair.

"What is it?" Jacob pulled his headphones off and shouted at his brother in indignation.

"Just move it." Travis said. The brothers came to the living room to find their parents exactly where they left them. Mom still on the couch and Dad still drinking in the kitchen.

Travis stood defiantly in the middle of the room, the photo album tucked under one arm and his other hand placed on his hip. "Mom, Dad, you have some explaining to do." He said with as much confidence as he could muster. Shannon seemed to barely register. She blinked and her eyes shifted, but otherwise she showed no sign she'd heard him. "I found this in Jocy's room." Travis held out the photo album. He tossed it to the floor and slid it to his mother's feet. "What does it mean?"

Shannon turned slowly, and then her eyes snapped wide when she saw it. She picked it up, her hands trembled as she stared at the front cover, reading the gold imprinted letters over and over. "Ben," she said softly at first, and when no response came, she shouted, "BEN!"

"What?" his annoyed, slurred words came from the kitchen.

"Come here," she called, "we found something."

Ben came into the front room, still holding one half-drunk bottle of beer. He spotted the photo album in Shannon's hands and instantly sobered. "What is that doing down here?"

"I don't know." Shannon admitted. "Travis said he found it in Jocelyne's room."

"What's so special about it?" Jacob asked.

"It hold secrets," Ben set his beer on the counter, then sat beside his wife. "Secrets about Jocelyne."

"What kind of secrets?" Jacob continued his questions.

Ben sighed, then glanced over at Shannon, and nodded. "Alright boys, I'm going to level with you." He took the album and opened it to one of the wedding photos. "Jocelyne isn't actually your sister."

The boys stared at the pictures, absorbing the bombshell that had just dropped. "She's not?" Travis asked.

"No." Ben continued. "She's actually your cousin. These people in this picture, the people getting married, are her real parents."

"And this," Shannon said as she pointed to the woman in the photo, "is her mother, my sister. Clarisse."

"But how did she get this?" Ben leaned forward on his elbows. "We had that locked in a trunk in the attic – " He stopped when the realization hit. He smacked his palm against his forehead. "Dammit."

"What?" Shannon asked.

"A few days ago, on the night we announced our family vacation, I found the hallway ladder open." Ben admitted. "I thought it had just come loose, but I guess that was her."

Travis turned to Jacob. "That was the day she asked about the key."

"The key?" Ben snapped.

"It was this old looking key." Travis admitted. "We didn't even know what it was for."

"How did you boys get it?" Ben drilled them.

The boys' shoulders hunched as they turned away with shame. "We might've been snooping around, looking for batteries." Jacob confessed.

Ben groaned and pressed his hands against his forehead. "Well, that at least explains her tirade." He said. "But why was she looking for it in the first place?"

"Something must've set her off." Shannon said. "Something that made her want to find what was in that trunk." The family remained in silence for a short time, all looking down at the open photo album and the pictures. Shannon's eyes lit up with thought. "Unless," she muttered, "it was that man."

Ben turned to her. "Um?"

"That man, the school counselor who wanted to talk with her the night before." Shannon said. "He said he'd been sent by my sister."

"And we sent him away." Ben argued.

"But it's the only thing that makes sense." Shannon stated. "Do you think he had some other way to contact her?"

"Give me a minute," Travis ran down the hall to his room, and returned with Jocelyne's cell phone. He pressed the oval button and the lock screen appeared. He traced his finger across the screen in a design he'd seen Jocelyne perform a dozen times before and the phone unlocked. "I can look through her contacts and see if anything is different."

His parents moved aside to let him sit between them.

Everyone craned over Travis's shoulders as he opened Jocelyne's contacts and he scrolled through the names. "This one," he said and stopped scrolling. "Mr. Otto."

"That's the one." Ben almost hissed.

Travis opened the messages app and found a string of texts between Jocelyne and Mr. Otto starting the night he came to visit. The conversation was short, just an agreement to meet the next day at the food court in the mall. "This meeting was just before she asked us about the key."

"Give me that." He snatched the phone from Travis's hand and called the number.

Before the phone could ring, an automated voice chimed, "We're sorry. The number you are trying to reach is no longer in service," and the call ended.

"Dammit." Ben cursed. "The bastard already ditched his phone."

"There was another name just below that one," Travis said. "Someone named Shawn." He took the phone back and opened the other number. It had been added earlier that day, no calls and no texts.

"Call it," Ben said. "I want to know who he is."

Travis did as he was bid and called the number. He put the

phone on speaker as a dial tone hummed. At least this number was still in service.

A connection was made. The other end of the line crackled and a voice came from the speaker. "Hey, Seal girl," the voice of a teenage boy spoke, "what's up?"

"Who are you?" Ben demanded.

"Whoa, wait, who is this?" The boy's voice trembled and back peddled.

"Jocelyne's father," Ben answered. "What is your connection with my daughter?"

"Sir, I promise, I haven't done anything with her." The teenager stated. "I just met her earlier today. I was supposed to help her with some . . . swimming exercises."

"Swimming exercises, huh?" Ben pressed.

"I swear, that's all it was," Shawn stammered.

"Don't play coy with me, kid. I know what my daughter is." Ben cut through the pretense.

"You do?" Shawn asked. "You know she's a . . ."

"A selkie, yes." Ben confirmed.

"What's a selkie?" Travis turned to his brother. Jacob shrugged.

Ben lifted his gaze to address his sons. "We'll explain in a minute." He returned his attention to the phone. "So you were with Jocelyne earlier today."

"Yes, sir." Shawn answered.

"Was anyone else with her?"

"What's this all about?" Shawn asked, suddenly concerned. "Did something happen to Jocelyne? We told her to keep a hold of her seal skin and never lose sight of it."

"Who is this 'we'?" Ben asked.

Shawn answered without hesitation. "Me and Mr. Otto."

"Dammit!" Ben shouted. He jumped off the couch and stormed around the room. "I knew it, I knew it! That son of a bitch!"

"What's going on?" Shawn's voice came over the phone speaker. "What's happened to her?"

Shannon spoke for the first time since they made the phone call. "She's run away from home. She dove into the ocean and swam away, and we have no idea where she's gone."

"I'm sorry, who is this?" Shawn asked, confused by the new voice. "Are you her mom?"

"Yes," Shannon answered.

"That's strange. Earlier today, Otto mentioned something about her mom." Shawn said. "He said, like, her mom was still waiting to reunite with her."

A stern look of concern came over Shannon's face, soon followed by absolute determination. "I know where she's gone." She stood and headed off towards her bedroom. "If Jocelyne's going to meet her mother, then so am I."

"Mom?" Travis called after her. "What are you doing?"

"I'm not going to sit by and do nothing." She came back to the living room with a laptop tucked under her arm. "I know where Jocelyne is going, and I'm going after her."

"All of us," Ben said, and pulled his wallet from his jeans pocket. He slipped a credit card from its sleeve and handed it to Shannon.

"Mom, Dad, what are you doing?" Travis asked hanging up the phone.

"Boys, go back to your room and pack some things. We'll be in later to make sure you don't forget anything." Ben told them. "We're going on our vacation a little earlier than expected."

"Tomorrow morning is the earliest I can transfer our flights." Shannon said as she tapped away at the keyboard.

"That's fine." Ben said. "With any luck, she might be on the same plane as us."

"We can hope," Shannon said with a sad smile. "I'm going

up to the attic to get my 'coat'. I'm going to need it if we're going to find Clarisse."

"Alright. I'll check on the boys while you do that." Ben said leaning over to give Shannon a kiss.

With that said everyone headed off to accomplish their individual tasks. They didn't have much time and there was a lot to do before they got on the plane in the morning. Ben walked into the twins' room to see what they'd packed. Travis was throwing clothes into an open suitcase while Jacob sat there in what looked like shock.

"Do you need a hand?" Ben asked.

Jacob jolted startled by the sound of his father's voice and Travis grinned. "What I need is a leg, but I guess a hand wouldn't hurt."

Ben groaned. "That was terrible." He said motioning for Travis to sit down so he could check Travis' suitcase. "We're going to have to leave at four if we want to make it to the airport so we need to pack now if you want to get any sleep." Ben said folding the clothes in Travis' suitcase.

It didn't take long to sort out Travis' suitcase and start on Jacob's. Once he'd finished packing the boys' stuff he tucked them into bed and was about to head to his room to pack his own suitcase when Travis spoke "Do you think Jocy will be okay?" he asked.

"We're going to make sure Jocy's okay. Now go to sleep we've got a big day tomorrow." Ben said closing the door behind him.

ACKNOWLEDGMENTS

We have many people we need to thank for the making of this book. Let's start with Steve Ferchaud for his brilliant cover. Katy Azevedo for running the library Open Mic where we shared the story and for beta reading for us. Cathy Chase and the North State Writers for the critique group that gave feedback.

And most important of all, we'd like to thank Joselyn Neal for permission to use her name all those years ago.

Jocelyne's quest for the truth

will continue in . . .

Secrets

Across the

Sea

Hope Hill is an author, poet, and former foster child. Starting at the age of nine, she worked to overcome great adversity through writing to tell her story. Her works have been published in multiple magazines and anthologies, as well as her debut novel, *Dancing on the Ceiling*.

N. J. Hanson lives in Northern California. He is a member of the California Writer's Club, and has been writing seriously since high school. His love of science fiction and fantasy has lead him down this path with his first book, the award-winning *The Last Stand of the Dragon*, being released at the age of twenty-four.

www.ingramcontent.com/pod-product-compliance
Lightning Source LLC
Chambersburg PA
CBHW050942120626
46552CB00001B/335